Scribbles from The Hills

Volume I

Abergavenny Writing Group
Anthology

Published by Sharon Brace on behalf of the Abergavenny Writing Group.

Copyright © 2020 Sharon Brace

The Abergavenny Writing Group have asserted their right under the Copyright, Design and Patents Act 1988 to be identified as the authors of this work. Copyright for each story or poem is the property of its author.

All rights reserved. This book or any portion thereof may not be reproduced or used in any manner whatsoever without the express written permission of the publisher except for the use of brief quotations in a book review or scholarly journal.

First Edition: 2020

A catalogue record of this book is available from the British Library.

ISBN : 978-1-716-38891-0

Cover designs by Shirley Stopforth

TABLE OF CONTENTS

ACKNOWLEDGEMENTS 8
FOREWORD 9
CAROLYN ARTHURS 10
   A LETTER TO GEORGE 10
   AND LEARN TOO LATE 13
   AS FAR AS I KNOW 14
   BONFIRE NIGHT 16
   CHRISTMAS PRESS RELEASE 18
      PART ONE – CHRISTMAS IS CANCELLED 18
      PART TWO – TWENTY-FOUR HOURS LATER 20
   A CHRISTMAS WISH 21
      PART ONE – A CHRISTMAS LIST 21
      PART TWO - A GOVERNMENT THAT FOCUSSES ON SHRINKING THE WEALTH GAP 22
   LEWIS 24
   OLD AND RIGHTFULLY DYING 33
   ROCKY MOUNTAIN SUN 35
   THE DE RANCOURTS 36
   THE MEETINGS 38
      PART ONE - THEN 38
      PART TWO – NOW 41
   THE NURSERY 43
   TRAVELS IN EUROPE 48
      PART ONE 48
      PART TWO - THE CONSEQUENCE 50

WRITING HELPS ME TO… 51
VICKY BALLARD **52**
   A CHRISTMAS WISH 52
   THE CHRISTMAS LIST 54
TONY HARDY **56**
   A BEGINNING, A MIDDLE AND AN END 56
   ABOVE LLANTHONY PRIORY 60
   A BOX OF MEMORIES... 62
   AUSTERITY 64
   BEANZ MEANZ HEINZ... 66
      PART ONE – FROM THE OUTSIDE.................... 66
      PART TWO – ON THE INSIDE............................ 70
   CHRISTMAS – DARK AND LIGHT................................. 72
      PART ONE – DARK... 72
      PART TWO – LIGHT.. 74
   DEAD TOWN 75
   EULOGY 77
   FIRST DAY OF SPRING... 79
   GUY FAWKES NIGHT 82
   HOME... 86
   HOUSE OF FOOLS 88
   IN TIMES OF COVID 90
      PART ONE - ON THE OUTSIDE......................... 90
      PART TWO - ON THE INSIDE 92
      PART THREE - A TIME OF CHANGE................. 94
   LANTERN PARADE... 96

MOTHER'S DAY 98
NEVADA TRILOGY 100
   PART ONE - NEVADA BLACKTOP 100
   PART TWO - CAR WASH 101
   PART THREE - ACTING ON IMPULSE 102
ODE TO DYLAN AND EDDIE 104
ON REGENT'S CANAL 106
SUNDOWN 107
TASMANIA TRILOGY 109
   PART ONE - WINEGLASS BAY 109
   PART TWO - A TASMANIAN CHRISTMAS 111
   PART THREE - THE RESCUE 112
THE CALVARY AT ST YVES 114
THE FIRST DAY OF SPRING 117
THE MEN'S ROOM 119
TOO OLD TO ROCK AND ROLL 123
   PART ONE – ROCK AND ROLL NIGHTS, ROCK AND ROLL DAYS 123
   PART TWO - AUF WIEDERSEHEN, CONNIE 126
   PART THREE – A LETTER FROM BERLIN 128
   PART FOUR – CONNIE REPLIES 130
   PART FIVE - BOYS IN THE BAND 132
   PART SIX – SNAKE HIPS RETURNS 135
   PART SEVEN - BE MY VALENTINE 138
TYPEWRITER, POSSESSED 146
VEGANUARY 148
WHY I WRITE (ARTURO'S OPUS) 150

WHY I WRITE (PAST, PRESENT AND FUTURE) 152
KATYA MORGAN **155**
    IT'S AUTUMN AGAIN 155
    MOBY AND THE BEANS... 157
    MY FAVOURITE SEASON AS A CHILD 163
    WHAT LIES BENEATH 164
MARTIN STOPFORTH **166**
    AUTUMN MEMORIES 166
    AUTUMN'S OUTSIDE... 168
    CHRISTMAS IS LOOMING... 169
    "CHRISTMAS CANCELLED" SHOCK 172
    ENDLESS DAY 175
    GLUE... 177
    GUMBO PIE 179
    LEGS 186
    NEW YEAR RESOLUTIONS SYNDROME 188
    ORIGINAL SIN 190
    SHEDDIE ALERT.. 191
    SQUARE SUN 193
    THE RESOLUTIONS CONUNDRUM 195
    THE WAR TO END ALL WARS................................... 197
    THINGS CAN ONLY GET WORSE 199
    THREE STEPS TO CHRISTMAS HEAVEN 201
    WRITE TO KNOW YOURSELF 203
    YELLOW BRICK ROAD 205
JULIE TAYLOR **206**
    CHRISTMAS 206

DELIRIUM 207
USC TIWARI **211**
    THE DANCER 211
AND FINALLY, A GROUP EFFORT **215**
    CHRISTMAS WORKSHOP POEM 215

ACKNOWLEDGEMENTS

My heartfelt thanks to the group members who volunteered to make this anthology happen:

Martin Stopforth and Tony Hardy.

A very special thanks to local artist Shirley Stopforth for the amazing artwork.

Thanks also to Jemima Jones and Nikki Jones who have given the group such a cosy home.

If you would like more information on the group or have an interest in joining us, details can be found at

www.sharonbrace.com

or

https://www.monmouthshire.gov.uk/communitylearning/abergavennycommunitylearning/

FOREWORD

When we got together for the first session, almost exactly two years ago, I could only imagine that the publication of our first anthology would become a reality.

In the two years since then, the group has gone from strength to strength, occasionally in numbers but always in quality and creativity. Together, we have written about the secrets of London and the humanitarian crisis in the Middle East. We have pictured the Autumn and what it means to each of us, exposed the horrors of the Gunpowder Plot and become reacquainted with friends and lovers from wartime. We have evoked childhood memories whilst revisiting the past. Some of us have met fears, expressed emotions, embraced catharsis and written stories which have so often been spiced with more than a touch of self. We have even delighted in a day of Christmas writings and poems.

In this, the first of what I hope will be many Abergavenny Anthologies, members have submitted pieces which were inspired and often written during the sessions. Therefore, I consider this anthology to be a celebration of the varied and timeless work the group has produced during its initial two years.

My gratitude to everyone who has braved the elements – rain, hail and shine – to come along during the last two years as we took fledgling steps towards this achievement. I am humbled by your commitment and your creativity and, it is with bated breath I look forward to what more there is to come.

Sharon Brace,

Tutor, Abergavenny Writing Group.

CAROLYN ARTHURS

Born and brought up in South Wales, Carolyn Arthurs is a retired Headteacher of a Special School. She and her husband have a large extended family, spread around the world and they travel a lot visiting them. She is a keen hiker and mountain climber. Writing has always been part of her life and work, but it is only since retirement that she has started writing creatively.

A LETTER TO GEORGE

My dear George,

I hope you are keeping well, and life is settling down for you. I suspect it might be somewhat easier. It has been a hard time in the neighbourhood and hopefully it is easing now that Ronnie was put away in Cardiff gaol and Suzie has been left alone with the goats.

Well my life has certainly changed. I can't say for the best, yet but sometimes difference and change is good for pondering and rethinking what life is about. I am living in what most people would call a "mud hut." It is a house built of mud and straw bricks but because it is plastered with lime and mud and painted on the outside, it actually takes the form of a small bungalow. I was reminded of its mud constituents only last week when a water pipe in the roof burst and mud started pouring down the bathroom wall!

It is situated on the edge of the forest about two hundred yards from my son's larger "mud hut." Every morning I sit on the wooden veranda in the warm morning air, drinking my hill tribe coffee and listening to the strange bird sounds that are made by the colourful cousins of our thrushes and sparrows. There are ripe bananas and avocados in the garden and glorious, richly coloured flowers.

I expect you are already wondering whether I intend to stay here and see my days out on this veranda! No George, not even the deliciously refreshing gin and lime we have every evening will keep me here. I shall stay until life has settled down again for my son and his family and then move out of their lives and back into the role of the occasional visiting Granny - I am not yet ready to stay for a long time and drive them all potty. I don't want them to think of me as a burden.

So, in a couple of months' time I am planning to move to the frozen North for a while. I don't know if you remember Jude. From the Yukon. She has invited me to stay for a while and Ian will have finished work by then and join me up in a log cabin just outside Whitehorse. I should arrive there early in May, just as the river is beginning to unfreeze. The bears will be emerging hungry and the mosquitoes will be frantically breeding! I can see your face as you read that, George... it reads "not the life for me, Carolyn." But I know I shall enjoy the hiking and helping around Jude's cabin. And yes, the gin and lime in the evening over a game of Scrabble!

I hope to be back in South Wales by the end of next year when the guy renting our house will have moved out (I hope he is a personable and helpful neighbour). My guess is that much will have changed in the neighbourhood by then. People will have forgotten what Ronnie did and the goats will have reproduced and be keeping Suzie busy. Will you stay around or is your land becoming too much for you? How is your daughter and do you still see much of your grandchildren? Is Brian still rotating his crops? Is he bringing in lambs this year from Gloucestershire so he can sell them to Waitrose as "Welsh" lamb?

I look forward to hearing all your news. Please say 'Hi' to Suzie when you see her, and to Brian.

Look after yourself.

From Carolyn,

With love.

AND LEARN TOO LATE

I wish I'd been the studious type,

Who'd thought a lot and smoked a pipe.

I wish I'd listened more and read

And used the brain inside my head.

But no, it was to be my fate,

I always seemed to learn too late.

I wish I'd worked for every test

In science, maths and all the rest.

I wish I'd conformed and tried hard to behave

And been a cameraman with Blue Planet Dave.

But no, it was to be my fate,

I always seemed to learn too late.

I wish I'd been mature when young

And thought before using my arrogant tongue.

I might have made a first ascent

Of some unknown peak in far Tashkent.

But no, it was to be my fate,

I always seemed to learn too late.

AS FAR AS I KNOW

As far as I know, or, anyway, as far as I remember, I have always had a brain.

As far as I know I have used this brain to think and propel me through my life. It has always been there at the centre of my life. But it has always been somewhat of a moveable feast. And now it has become a feast that is slowly disintegrating through age.

I have become unsure of what I know and even more unsure of what I remember, and this has encouraged me to rely on what is called "poetic licence." In modern terms this is known as '"fake news." So, what I write following this must be taken with that pinch of salt.

As far as I know I had a carefree childhood until the age of twelve. Life was easy, relatively undisciplined, and outdoor based. As far as I know it was my brother not me, who lit a firecracker behind Farmer Pugh's cows in the lane. As far as I know it was me Farmer Pugh punished for it.

As far as I know it was me who was pushed through the ice into the freezing canal on the way home from school, and it was my brother who eventually rescued me when the culprits ran off. I remember that I was punished and not the culprits.

As far as I remember, I once watched as my brother (as part of a large group of protestors) was arrested at an Anti-Vietnam rally in Grosvenor Square, outside the U.S. embassy. Released later that day, we slunk back to the flat and decided we would never tell our parents. Of course, we did, but much later in life when we were both upstanding members of society.

In this digital age these anecdotes would have been instantly recorded and posted on Instagram or Facebook. A host of phone users would have seen the cows stampeding down the lane and maybe even known I was grounded for a week. Someone would have seen me waving and flailing and slipping and grabbing as I tried to crawl out of the canal.

Maybe someone would have seen who pushed me in. Thousands would have seen my brother pulled by the police and pushed into a van.

BONFIRE NIGHT

Ponty Observer 7/11/2018

Ponty Observer enquiry unveils extraordinary deceit at village fireworks party.

Police were yesterday searching the Black Mountains for an unusual piece of stolen property.

As Pontyclun Village Annual Guy Fawkes celebration took place the night before last, in the field above Neuadd Farm, thieves broke into the farmhouse and stole the mattress from Farmer Jones' double bed.

'It was our biggest bonfire yet,' Pontyclun's Mayor told us, 'and we had more fireworks than ever before. I can see how no-one noticed what was happening in the farmhouse. The village was transfixed by what was in the air, and the noise was terrific.'

In an interview with the investigating Police Officer, the Ponty Observer was told that no vehicle was involved in the burglary. The thieves took off on foot with the mattress and appeared to have left through the farmyard at the back of the house, in the direction of Twmpath Hill. Twmpath Hill is well known for being a particularly wild and deserted area of moorland, with no houses for some miles around. Police told us that they believed there were at least four members in the gang who carried out the crime, as four sets of footprints had been found in the mud in the farmyard. Nothing else in the house had been touched. The Investigating Officer expressed surprise that the gang had walked past a number of valuable antique pieces to get to the mattress.

'We've come to a bit of a full stop,' said the Officer.

Farmer Jones was unavailable for interview. However, his wife said he had left the farm on the previous day and she had not heard from him. Mrs Jones was willing to speak to us and to explain what turned out to be a perplexing story of deceit. The mattress, we were told, was not filled with flock, or polypropylene pieces, or feathers, or even straw, but with fifty-pound notes that had been stuffed in, one by one, over the last fifteen years by Farmer Jones himself.

'I had no idea he was doing this,' Mrs Jones said. 'Hill farming doesn't bring in much money and so we were always short, and now he's buggered off for good with a mattress full of all our savings.'

So, what is the story behind this skulduggery? Farmer Jones was last seen at Bristol Airport in an EasyJet queue for Geneva with a large backpack. Next to him, a tall blonde woman in a shiny fur coat.

CHRISTMAS PRESS RELEASE

PART ONE – CHRISTMAS IS CANCELLED

Shock and horror reigns over us all, as Christmas is cancelled.

The future of Christmas looked uncertain last night as news emerged that Santa had tended his resignation. The news flash was released by the Conservative Party on the eve of the controversial Parliamentary Brexit vote.

The Prime Minister, speaking outside Number 10, told waiting journalists that she had heard from the Department of Gifts and Handouts (formally the DWP) that the Minister, Sant Aclause, had resigned, for what she described as "personal reasons." She hinted that, in effect, this would almost certainly mean that Christmas was cancelled.

Our Christmas correspondent has more recently heard from those working in the department. The reasons, he was told, were an ongoing dissatisfaction, uncertainty, and lack of staff.

'Recently, European Christmas workers have left for better paid jobs. They have just swanned off to the larger European Countries,' he was told by a remaining on-site worker.

The impact of this will be huge. It is a crisis that has already begun to spread frenetic activity throughout the nation. Schools have closed, town and village halls have been boarded up, and lights have been switched off.

When asked if Christmas could merely be shifted to a later date, the Prime Minister stared blankly and turned to walk back in to Number 10.

PART TWO – TWENTY-FOUR HOURS LATER

Today's Parliamentary vote, and the resulting wave of response from the media and, indeed, the nation, has brought hope to millions of children across the country.

The Prime Minister, speaking outside the Houses of Parliament, told the waiting press that, as a result of the overwhelming support for the plan to ditch Brexit and re-establish normal relations with the EU, Christmas was back on the books.

The Prime Minister stated that she had appointed a new Minister for Gifts and Handouts, someone who better reflected the diverse nature of Britain's population. She added that Christmas was to be reinstated, and she had given an extra ten million pounds to the Department for bigger and better gifts, and handouts for children under fifteen and adults over sixty-five.

Across Britain it was another day of frenetic activity. Schools opened, church bells rang, and towns and villages restored their Christmas decorations.

Finally, the forecast for the weather over Christmas is six inches of snow on Christmas Eve, and bright sunshine throughout the day.

A CHRISTMAS WISH

PART ONE – A CHRISTMAS LIST

Dear Father Christmas,

If I thought you were able to fly in and fulfil the following list, I would surely believe in you, and probably in God, too. In fact, if you come up with the goods, I will wear a hat and start attending Sunday services.

    Firstly, my family. Please keep them all safe, well, and happy.

    Secondly, my own bucket list. Please will you arrange for me to summit a four-thousand-metre mountain in the Alps this coming summer. I am willing to train for it. I'd be grateful if you would drop in all the necessary "gear."

    Finally, general requests. Please empty the sea of that ghastly plastic Sir David Attenborough keeps reminding us about and allow us to start again, using a much more sensible approach. And while I'm on the subject of climate change, I loved the weather last summer. And are you able to reverse the Brexit vote and give us a Government that focuses on shrinking the wealth gap?

Thanks, in anticipation,

Carolyn.

PART TWO - A GOVERNMENT THAT FOCUSSES ON SHRINKING THE WEALTH GAP

The Council Offices are very busy this month. It's Christmas again and a lot has happened to some of the folks in this small Welsh town.

"ere's my form,' she said. 'See, I was laid off because sales have gone down, and I was the last person employed in the factory. I applied for Universal Credit, but it hasn't come through yet, and I have no money left.'

The tall woman handed her four large carrier bags crammed with food stuff.

'That's why we have a Foodbank, love. Shit happens. Here you go, have this.'

She moved on to the next in the queue.

'I lost my job. I came in late two days in a row and that was it.'

She looked at the young man.

'What was the job?' she asked.

'Car cleaning at the carwash place.' He handed her his form.

'Have you applied for Universal Credit?' she asked.

'Can't,' he said. 'I don't have a computer and they can't give me an appointment at the Job Centre till next week.'

She handed him four large carrier bags crammed with food stuff and nodded to the next in the queue.

This is what it's like if you are near the bottom of the British pile. Please Santa: give us a Government that focuses on shrinking the wealth and poverty gap.

LEWIS

I met Jules on the Western coast of France. Mel and I had driven down there after leaving Uni.

'We'll get a job,' Mel had said optimistically. She was right. Mel washed dishes in a small café, and I sold sugared peanuts to the sunbathers.

'Choux choux,' I shouted as I walked up and down the crowded beach.

We shared a boss - Madame Mere. She seemed to have a franchise on much of the beach activity and even the campsite where we stayed.

I first noticed Jules striding down the beach with a group of surfers carrying their boards towards the sea. He was tall and stood out from the others because of his bleached straw-like hair (ruined by the salt and sun, my mother would say). All day they surfed and hung around the tide line, waiting for the right wave at the right time. Then I noticed him again. He was staying in a white van not far from our tent. At the end of the day he would wash in the cold shower at the edge of the sand, and eventually emerge from his van wearing black trousers and a white shirt. He worked most evenings as a waiter in another of Madame Mere's establishments – a more "up market" restaurant in the town.

Our relationship developed over the summer. His English was pretty good, and my French was passable. He was quiet and thoughtful, sometimes to the extent that I thought he was depressed. He was unlike the other surfers who were drinkers and party goers. When we weren't working or surfing, we walked the wind-blown Atlantic coastline, along endless, white, sandy beaches. We walked to other towns and sat in cafés, talking, and finding out about each other. Having said that, it was he who found out about me. A mist seemed to hang around his childhood. His mother had died when he was young, and he had never known who his father was, so he had been brought up by an aunt and uncle in Normandy. I never found out what they did, but Jules went to school and didn't do very well. I thought he was clever. He had a mind that could work its way around any machine and fingers that matched his brain. He could fix absolutely anything. Madame Mere recognised this and used him as an odd job person. He fixed a cistern in the wash block, the generator at the back of the beach cafe, the engine of Mel's car, Monsieur Mere's iPad - the list was endless.

By the end of August, the tourists started to drift away. Mel and I had planned to leave early in September because she had a job to go back to in a small solicitors in Newport. Mel had done well in her law degree. I didn't have a job to go back to. I was an only child and had lived with my mother until I went to Uni. We lived in a small town up in the Ebbw Valley. Mam was a single parent and worked as a teaching assistant in the Primary School. We had a close relationship. I spoke to her a couple of times a week. Who or where my father was, I had never known.

'Why don't you stay here and work for Madame Mere?' asked Jules. 'We could live in the van until it gets cold and then find an apartment.'

It was then I made the first decision that was to change my life. I rang my mother.

'I'm not comin' 'ome with Mel, Mam.'

'Oh my God, why not?' she asked.

'Well, it's Jules, Mam. He's asked me to stay and I think I am in love.'

'Don't be so daft, girl, you've only known 'im six weeks.' she replied.

I stayed. A life changer.

We found a small ground floor flat owned by Madame Mere in the town. I worked as a waiter in her restaurant and Jules worked as a caretaker and odd job person for all her properties. Mine was often shift work so that some days we only saw each other in passing. But we saw enough of each other to build on our relationship and prove my mother wrong. I did love him, and I believed that he loved me. He was warm, kind, gentle, easy, and fun, but I didn't really know about him - where he had been, or what he had done before we met. He was an enigma, albeit an attractive and loveable one. It didn't matter that much, I suppose, but I was curious about his history and what might have shaped this quietly thoughtful person I had come to know so intimately. When I pressed him to talk about himself, he would shrug his shoulders and say that his life had been much of the same; he had worked in various parts of France, doing a variety of jobs.

So, that was how our lives progressed through the winter. There were some changes though - mainly financial changes - and they began one evening when Jules came home with a new laptop.

'Where did you get the money from?' I asked.

He shrugged. 'My Aunt sent it for my birthday.'

'Birthday! When was that?'

From then on there were more and more changes. He spent hours on eBay and we slowly filled up the garage and apartment with "stuff"; a bicycle for me, a camera, a new surfboard, a canoe, a kite surfer, a wetsuit, and so on.

'Where did you get the money from?' I asked again and again.

'Tips from Madame Mere's tenants and clients.'

'Madame Mere has given me a rise.'

'A guy in town owed me two hundred Euros from the summer.'

'I've been saving it.'

I learned how to shrug and not bother about it - it was easy really. So, we just got on with our lives.

At Christmas time we went home to South Wales. Mam was excited and I was dying to see her. We hitched to Cherbourg and went across as foot passengers. As we rode through Normandy, I asked which part he had grown up in.

'In the country. East of Lisieux,' was his vague reply.

Christmas at home was great. Two weeks of my Mam's cooking, visits with cousins, aunts, uncles, friends, and a night out with Mel in Cardiff. Jules was loved by everyone who met him, charming my mother in his quiet way. Helping her. Fixing and servicing every broken appliance in the house, including her ancient Sony sound system, computer mouse, food mixer, and so on. Then moving on to do the same in various other family members' houses in the terrace.

I was sad to leave them all, but having made a decision to live in France, I couldn't go back to Wales and could never leave Jules. The return journey was not so good. I felt sick on the bus all the way to Portsmouth and then vomited my way across the Channel. We got a lift in a lorry as far as Bordeaux, and then caught a bus to the coast. I was still feeling sick.

It took a few weeks before I realised that I was pregnant. It was a shock to us both. Jules shrugged his shoulders and said it was fine by him. I took that as a Jules-style commitment statement. So, another life changer, but this time an irreversible one.

Lewis Jacques Jones was born in the local hospital. Jules was with me, and Mam was waiting in the flat surrounded by a pile of hand knitted hats, cardigans and blankets she had brought from home. Lewis was a long-legged, pink, scrawny baby with wisps of blond hair like his father's. He cwtched up to me as I fed him, and my life gently changed into something so different from anything I had ever experienced. Mam stayed a month and got to know her grandson, and looked after us, cooking every evening and keeping the flat clean. While she was with us, Jules took a couple of weeks off working from the Paper Mill in town and from his odd jobs with Madame Mere and drove every day to a place called Dune de Pyla, to learn how to paramotor.

'Paramotor,' my mother cried, 'what in God's name is that? What do you want to be doing with that, Jules?' She had seen the garage full of activity gear; the surf boards, sea kayaks, wet suits, kite surfer, and now a paramotor.

'It is a paraglider with a small portable motor, Glynis,' he told my mother. 'You can fly over hills and out over the coast and sea, free like a bird.'

'Well, I don't know where you get all that stuff in the garage or how you can afford it, but it doesn't seem very sensible, Jules. You don't wanna be flying like a bird when you're a father.'

Jules looked hurt.

'Glynis, I take the responsibility of my son with thought and care. I will provide for him and for Kath.'

They didn't talk about it again. Jules carried on travelling every day and returning home every evening. When he was with us, he took an interest in Lewis and cuddled and cwtched him, but it didn't seem like much of a bonding process to me.

Mam left at the end of the month. She had enjoyed living with us and had even spent time with Madame Mere, who spoke a Pidgin English that rivalled my mother's limited French. Jules finished his paramotor course and was back working at the Paper Mill.

It was a mild winter, and we didn't go back to Wales for Christmas, but planned a longer holiday for the spring. Jules was keen to try out the paramotor and had read that Scotland had good wind and stretches of beach that matched the wind direction. We left in April, somewhat hastily, not even managing to say our goodbyes to Madame Mere. Jules finished his job at the mill, and we left one night in the van, which was now kitted out for camping. The paramotor was strapped onto the back.

We went to stay with Mam for a couple of weeks and parked outside the house. It was Lewis' first trip to Wales, and he was adored by all my relatives. He had a shock of blonde hair and piercing blue eyes. He was a lively and responsive baby and blossomed with the attention of all the family members.

I wanted to stay longer but Jules was keen to move on, so we set off and travelled up to Glasgow. From there we drove up the west coast. Whenever we found what Jules deemed to be a suitable site, we stopped for a few days and Jules tried out the paramotor. Lewis and I would watch him struggle along the grass as he attempted to take off. The blade that was strapped to his back was heavy and he had to run with it holding onto the straps of the sail above him. It looked impossible to take off and often he didn't manage it.

The wind needed to be strong enough to lift him but not too strong to blow him about. The visibility had to be good. On clear sunny days he could sometimes get a thermal that would lift him higher and further. When he did, he would circle and climb gently up as he headed out over the sea, gradually gaining height. Sometimes we would lose sight of him. He would stay out for a couple of hours and eventually we would hear the throb of the motor returning. Landing looked easier because gravity was on his side, but he would often fall under the weight of the machine and the pull of the wind. It was an obsession. It seemed dangerous to me, but I understood the appeal of sailing over the land and sea like a bird.

We eventually drove over to the Isle of Skye, staying in a couple of places and then up to Uig, where we caught the ferry to the Outer Hebrides. Harris was empty and wild. We drove along the coast where there were rocky inlets and bleached beaches. We camped in Hushinish (the end of the road), at a site that looked across to the Isle of Scarp and then way beyond across the Atlantic to Northern Canada. There was a small field between two beaches. Jules liked the look of it. You could run north to south, or east to west, depending on the wind direction. The weather was beautiful, but the wind was variable – it would change direction and pick up speed on an unpredictable whim.

Jules watched it carefully and we swam and played on the beach and walked over the rocks carrying Lewis. It was a quiet thoughtful time for Jules, and I put his mood down to his obsession. And then one morning we woke to perfect conditions - a steady southerly wind, sun, patchy cloud, and warmth. Jules spent an hour in preparation, dressing and harnessing himself. Then Lewis and I went out to the field to watch his take off. He took a few runs at it. The wind seemed to be changing, but finally he lifted off the ground and circled up higher and higher. We waved. At first, he seemed to be searching for a thermal over the land, but then the wind changed, and he drifted north and west out over the ocean. Lewis and I had breakfast and then went down to the beach. There was no sign of Jules now and I idly wondered which way he had gone. I tried phoning him but there was no reply - not unusual given the variable signals in such a remote place.

After a couple of hours, we returned to the van for lunch. I tried calling Jules again. This time the phone rang... in the van, in his coat pocket! It was so unlike him to forget something. After lunch, Lewis and I walked out along the path that followed the coastline. The weather by now had changed and it had become windier and colder. We looked and listened. Nothing. Another life changer.

Air Sea Rescue, Police, and locals all helped and searched. I was questioned and interviewed. Jules had disappeared into thin air. We stayed in Hushinish for some time. Every day, Lewis and I would walk along the coast in the hope of finding something. I wasn't sure what sort of something, but anything to tell me what might have happened. Jules wasn't found and I eventually drove back to Wales with Lewis. There was no body, so I could not believe that he was dead. I was sure he was still alive. Mam was devastated, as were the rest of the family. I kept on believing that he would walk into the house. Every time the phone rang, I knew it would be the Scottish Police.

After some months, I left Lewis with Mam and returned to France to clear out our apartment. Mel took time off work and came with me. We met with Madame Mere, who had been interviewed by the Highlands and Islands Police (the French speaking branch, no doubt). I told her I believed that Jules was alive. I had no reason to believe otherwise. She was subdued and reluctant to talk about Jules. She was surprised when I offered her the owed rent (Mam had lent it to me before I left). When I opened the door to our apartment, I was overcome by grief. I sat down at the table and wept. I wept because I missed Jules. Because I was lonely without him. Because we had spent a short, intense, intimate, and harmonious time together and I missed that. Did I really believe that he was still alive or was that part of how I was coping with what was (to those around me) inevitable?

We cleared up, sold, and gave away much of what we found in the flat. It was Mel who found a stash of letters and bills in a shoe box under a pile of wetsuits. When I started looking through them, I was stunned. They were unpaid bills and letters demanding money. They were the bills for all the "stuff in the garage", as my mother had called it. Then there were bills and demands from years before. In all, I was looking at debts of more than €150,000. Then finally at the bottom of the box was the biggest eye opener of all. Two documents. One was a birth certificate for someone called Jean Paul Louvet, born in Belgium, mother Marie Therese, father unknown. The second one was an old passport, with a picture of Jules in earlier times. He had neatly cut dark hair and a name that I did not recognise, born in Marseilles, nationality French.

So, when I got home to Wales, I was sure of two things. Firstly, Jules was alive and, secondly, I would never see him again.

OLD AND RIGHTFULLY DYING

We will all be there round your bed, Mum,

When you're old and are ready to go.

We will weep and look sombre and sad, Mum,

Like Dickens would put in his prose.

I'm ready to leave right away, dear,

They'd finish a dog off in my state.

I'm useless and dependent on you, dear,

I'm ready to face up to my fate.

You are fun and entertaining, Mum,

You have stories we all love to hear.

We don't want you to fall off your perch yet,

We are happy to do all the care.

I'm afraid that my time has come dear,

I am old and am rightfully dying.

Don't grieve or worry about me, dear,

When you've done with all that crying.

I'll be here in all that you see, dear,

In your days and your nights and your dreams.

I'll be found in all nooks and corners, dear,

For nothing appears as it seems.

She lay back and closed her brown eyes,

And we sat round the bed and we cried.

She was right in her final pronouncement,

She always was right, we sighed.

ROCKY MOUNTAIN SUN

I look up and watch a creeping glow

That spreads itself over the crest of the glistening crags.

It moves slowly and tries to grasp and claim each peak,

Creating shadows.

This icon of life's necessity seems reluctant in this cold land.

Does it feel it can't win? Has it lost the battle?

Silently, and with little warning

It starts its' steady climb into the clear sky.

Giving light and trying hard to warm us.

The battle is won.

It enlists the support of the surrounding snow

To reflect and enhance its offering to life.

Is this the same sun that encourages me

As I plant the garden in spring?

Is this the same sun that burns my neck

As I hike those green slopes to reach the peaks and crags?

No reluctance, no battle now.

Just the full blasting heat of the summer sun.

THE DE RANCOURTS

When I was eighteen, I went to Paris to live with a family in order to improve my French. I was erroneously called an "au pair", which I was never too sure of as there was no job description. Maybe "au pair" means slave, I thought. No, it actually means on a par or equal - phew!

The rich, decadent, aristocratic family I lived with were called the de Rancourts. Monsieur worked for Paris Match and Madame worked in the home, bringing up her three children (aged nine, eleven and thirteen) and maintaining a level of cleanliness I had never come across living in the Welsh valleys.

I was employed to look after the children. This involved producing breakfast, walking with them to and from school, providing teatime snacks, room cleaning, and teaching them English. The rest of the day was my own time to explore Paris. So, I did feel on a par or equal, except that I didn't have much money, so got to know Paris on foot.

The de Rancourts were determined I should be part of their family. We ate together, travelled together, and prayed together. Every evening we sat round the fireplace, with the shiny Madonna effigy above it. They prayed devoutly. I watched with interest as the children poked and pinched each other and the parents slapped them. I came from a family of atheists where rules were fairly slack and corporal punishment was unknown. These children were used to being hit for what seemed the most trivial of sins. I felt sorry for them. But they were not cowed or frightened; they just carried on with their trivial sinning.

Being a member of the family, however, did not stretch to the time when we visited the family chateau where grand-mère lived. This was a vast house in beautiful grounds south of the city. Grand-mère was resolute that I was a servant, not an on-a-par being. She was rather disdainful of me and certainly failed on the inclusion ticket. My sleeping quarters were in the East wing of the house, in a small room next to Marie Therèse. Marie Therèse was actually the paid "live-in" servant, and in many ways reminded me of mad Bertha Mason in Jane Eyre - you know the one who finally burnt the house down! She taught me how to lay the table - cutlery face down to show the family crest. She taught me how to wash up - glasses first, then cutlery, plate, etc. Friendly though she was, I locked my bedroom door every night.

So, yes, I learnt a more fluent version of my A-Level French, and I got to know the art galleries, parks, and open spaces of Paris. But I was quite lonely, and never really felt relaxed, or very loving towards the de Rancourt family.

THE MEETINGS

PART ONE - THEN

Maggie came out of the hospital gates and turned towards the east, walking quickly towards her digs. It was dark and the streets were unlit, and wet from the day's rain. She always felt nervous getting back alone. Nervous of the groups of drunken servicemen she sometimes met. They would shout and lunge at her and she always had to run.

    She had been in London since 1915 and now, a year on, she was nearing the end of her training as a nurse and nearing the time when she would be sent to the front. It had been a long and painful journey getting to London from the Forest of Dean. Convincing her middle class, mine-owning parents that she wanted to train as a nurse and work where she was needed, had taken its toll. Her mother could barely speak to her civilly anymore, and her letters had been few and far between, terse and cold. But Maggie had been determined and here she was walking steadily through the grimy streets of east London, avoiding anyone she saw.

    The War, they were told, was going strategically well and the forces were fighting in the Somme. Little news filtered through to her. Her main source of information was from her brother Arthur, who was at the front in the Royal Army Ordnance, as a staff sergeant. He was a gunsmith, and he worked in the trenches and behind the front repairing artillery. He had told her that there were many dead and injured and that nurses were needed, which had spurred her on to complete what her mother had wanted to deny her.

    She was almost at her digs now. She rounded the corner into Sydney Street and walked towards the Sailors Arms, where there was noise and bright lights. As she neared the pub, she stepped off the pavement to avoid being too near the action. There was a soldier sitting alone on the curb. He looked up at her as she passed by. She looked at him. There was a moment of recognition.

'Billy?' she said. 'Billy Pugh?'

The soldier smiled broadly and stood up. He looked at her.

'Maggie! The Coal Merchant's daughter!'

'What are you doing here? she questioned. 'How come you are in uniform?'

'Same reason as you, I guess, looking at your uniform. There is a bloody war going on Maggie!'

She stared hard at him.

'But Billy, you can only be sixteen years of age.'

'Yep, that's it Maggie, I joined up in Gloucester, when I was fourteen and looking eighteen, and nobody batted an eyelid. They just want two arms, two legs and not much of a brain, and I fit that bloody bill. And no-one never questioned me.'

They were not the same age. They were not the same social class. But they had gone to the same elementary school, and Billy and his family had lived in the street behind the large Victorian coal merchant's house. And here they were, involved in the same war. On a level footing, thought Maggie.

'So, what has it been like for you so far, Billy?' she asked tentatively.

He looked at her warm, open face.

'Bloody mad,' he replied. 'It's run by mad men and we are mad doing as they say, and none of us knows why we are there anymore, and the bloody Germans probably don't know, neither.'

PART TWO – NOW

WW1 PARTICIPANTS

As part of our WW1 Armistice Commemoration, we at the BBC, are looking for participants who served in WW1 to join us in talking about their experiences on, and behind, the front.

If you have memories you are willing to share with us on screen, please contact us on 0800 234 5499.

Maggie had seen this ad in the Radio Times and rung the number. A fresh-faced young journalist had been to visit her in her ground floor flat in Cardiff. She had sensitively asked Maggie questions about her time as a nurse at Ypres. Maggie, a relatively lively minded ninety-year-old, living alone but next door to her daughter, was interested in the project and willing to tell her what she remembered of her time. After seventy years it was still painful to recall some of the events. She knew that many participants had struggled all their lives to talk about the war that was erroneously called the Great War. When the journalist, named Jane, asked if she would join some others in a TV special to be recorded at the BBC Wales studios, she said 'yes' out of interest mainly, to see what other people had to say, and to meet others of her generation, of whom there were very few left.

  A taxi fetched Maggie the following week and drove her to the studios in Llandaff. She had taken a long time to dress but, in the end, she chose her pale blue cashmere, her pearls and a plaid skirt. When she looked in the mirror at herself, she sighed. Her white hair needed cutting. In fact, she thought, 'I need a complete makeover really, no hope of that!'

The studio was a comfortable area of chairs and small tables. She had arrived first and, placing her walking stick under her chair, sat down, and waited. People started arriving. She noticed a man in a wheelchair arriving. His hair was thick and white, his skin wrinkled and tanned, and he had a row of medals on his lapel. He looked familiar, but then her attention was drawn to the presenter of the programme, who was introducing himself and had started going round the group as an introduction. When it came to the man in the wheelchair, he cleared his throat. 'My name is William Pugh, I come from Cinderford in the Forest of Dean, and I served in what was known as Kitchener's Army, at the Somme and then Ypres.'

She stared at him. Yes, yes, yes, it was Billy Pugh, whom she had seen outside the pub on Sydney Street all those years ago! They had met twice in the days following and had talked about the war and their childhoods! Maggie had never seen him or heard from or of him since.

'Billy,' she said, 'Billy Pugh.' She walked across to his wheelchair, bent down, and held both his hands in hers. Her eyes watered. 'I thought you were dead. I thought you had been killed at Ypres.'

He looked up at her. Her face was warm and gentle as he remembered it.

'I bloody survived it all, Maggie.'

'We both did, Billy.'

THE NURSERY

'Just these, please,' said Cerys, handing him the tray of plants. It was late in the day and she was on her way home from work. It had been a lovely warm day and she felt inspired to get her garden going.

'Sure Ma'am, my pleasure,' he replied in a strange, southern US drawl. She stared at him. He looked sort of American. A baseball cap reversed on a large GI shaven head; a couple of chains around his neck; a vest that shouted "South Dakota sucks" on it; and striped Bermuda shorts.

'How much are the pelargoniums?' she asked.

'Like, Mom charges two pounds a tray, but you can have them for a pound fifty.'

He answered in his soft-spoken drawl. He didn't look at her when he spoke and was standing rather close to her. She felt slightly uncomfortable.

'Thank you,' she murmured, watching him more closely as he placed the pots in a tray. How odd to find a southern American here in the heart of South Wales, running a Nursery. Her thoughts were suddenly interrupted by a scream from the other end of the long greenhouse.

'*Ronald*, where the bloody 'ell did you put them grandiflora petunias?'

'No American drawl there,' she thought, 'Welsh valleys through and through.'

'In the cold frame, out the back, Mom, honey.' His reply to this verbal tirade was gentle and sweet - almost sugary, she thought. Ronald took her money and carried the plants to her car. She watched him. He was a tall, heavy man, probably around forty years old.

Ronald's mother always cooked them tea at seven. It was Tuesday, which meant it was sausage and chips. When he entered the small house, it was gone seven-fifteen and his mother was angry (again).

'You'll drive me round the bloody bend you will. I'm sick of yer bloody time-keepin'.'

'Sorry mother,' Ronald murmured.

'Sorry doesn't make any bloody sense in your book my boy. An' stop talkin' in that bloody daft voice.'

Ronald sat down and looked at his plate. 'Hmmm, just love this tea, Mom, any ketchup?'

Ronald and Mattie Jones had run the Nursery since Gwil (Ronald's father) had died suddenly four years ago. Ronald had taken over all the heavy-duty jobs around the site. His mother did most of the customer service. Ronald was a big, heavy, slow-moving man. He had a stoop, as though his overflowing gut put a strain on his body. When he wasn't wearing a baseball cap, he wore a bandana round his head. He was someone who was happy in his own company and his own thoughts, and his thoughts were almost entirely concerned with all things American. He had never visited the United States, only in his dreams and via his computer. He watched endless movies about the Wild West, about gangsters, about small-town America. Anything really as long as it was about, and made in, America. This was an obsession that he now carried through to his everyday existence. He had always had obsessions of some sort, but this one had started some years ago and didn't seem to be waning yet.

'The Doctor at the Surgery said my bloated gut and tiredness was all down to constipation and diet,' said his Mother, watching him shovel in his chips. 'He sent me to the dietician this morning.' Ronald was barely listening. 'Talked about vegetables, pulses and seeds. Bollocks to that I thought. But she gave me some free samples. Said I should mix 'em in with all foods.'

Ronald looked at the packets in the centre of the table.

'Looks like they belong in a flowerpot.' He picked up a packet labelled "Linseed." 'They look familiar,' he said thoughtfully, pouring some onto his palm. He put them back on the table.

Ronald watched TV that night - a gangster movie about Chicago in the 1920s. Then he sat in front of his computer and watched a road movie made in 1989. Then he trawled the net for reviews and articles about Chicago in the 1920s and California in the 1980s. He often did this - long Google research sessions following a movie. He searched and found out about every detail that interested him. He knew the names and details of places, streets, guns, historical events. What people did, why they did it and how they did it - a constructed fantasy world, sometimes loosely based on history. He finally went to bed at three a.m.

At seven-thirty his mother was at his door yelling at him. He felt tired and reluctant to get up, but she was insistent, and it was an easier option to conform than face more of her ranting. He was able to tolerate his mother's anger most of the time. But sometimes it became too much to bear, and he would lose his cool with her and fight back with mean words and violent tones. These times made him feel worse not better. He believed his mother hated him. He believed she blamed him for the death of his father. It had been Ronald who had left two full watering cans at the top of the steps outside the big greenhouse. It had been Ronald who had left the cardboard box of broken windowpanes at the bottom of the steps. His father had died in hospital two days after the fall.

Breakfast was coffee and a peanut butter sandwich. He sat opposite his mother, feeling irritated and angry at her.

'These are what the Dietician gave me.' she said, emptying a packet of cereal into her bowl. 'Free from the Welsh Assembly no doubt, taken fresh from their bleedin' bird feeders by the looks.'

He watched her shake some of the flax seeds over the cereal, and then she poured on milk and took her first mouthful.

'Hmmm. Tropical bollocks I calls that. They lives well, them assembly birds. Here's the list for today,' she said, passing Ronald a scrappy piece of paper.

'Mind you do them 'anging baskets by eleven. I'll be off to Lidl then.'

He took the list and silently shuffled out of the room.

When he arrived at the largest of the green houses, he looked at the list: Pricking out; potting on; watering; pruning; collecting seeds (they did a lot of that to save money); spraying, and then there was the hanging baskets for the local supermarket - they needed a lot of TLC. He started with the hanging baskets and then moved onto watering. As he walked along the greenhouse beds with the hose pipe, he noticed the Laburnums had gone to seed. He picked off a pod and opened it. The small black seeds inside looked like his mother's addition to her cereal. He took out a small envelope from his pocket and emptied the seeds into it and then harvested the rest of the pods and did the same.

His mother left for Lidl with the hanging baskets and Ronald went into the house to get himself a coffee. He sat down at the kitchen table and reached into his pocket for the seeds he had collected. He poured them out onto the patterned oilcloth that covered the table. Then he took a packet of the dietician's seeds and poured them out next to the laburnum. They looked pretty similar. Suddenly the phone rang.

'Gwil's Nursery, how can I help you,' he drawled.

'You forgot to put the trailing lobelia in those bloody baskets,' yelled his mother. 'They won't accept them and it's your bloody fault. I'm sick to death of you and yer daft bloody brainless 'ead.' She slammed the phone down. Ronald wandered slowly out to finish his list of jobs. It wasn't looking good for the rest of the day.

It was a chilly damp Saturday morning. Cerys was sitting with her husband in their kitchen, drinking tea and browsing the Ponty Observer.

'Good God, Bryn,' she said. 'They've closed Gwil's Nursery. The old woman died.'

'Oh yeah?' answered Bryn.

Cerys continued 'The Coroner said it was death by misadventure. Ate something poisonous. Well, there must be a lot of dodgy chemicals in them places. Never liked 'er much - she 'ad a mouth like a sewer. I expect 'er son'll go back to the States. I think that's where he was born.'

TRAVELS IN EUROPE

PART ONE

At the age of nineteen, in 1966, I was a student in London. My then boyfriend (and now aged husband) and I saved our money throughout the year from our student grants and bought return air tickets to Rome. We had chosen to hitchhike around Italy for the six weeks of our summer holidays. Our canvas/leather backpacks were carefully packed with a sleeping bag, a plate, a penknife, a raincoat, and a couple of books - not much else other than scant clothing.

At the age of nineteen, in 1999, my youngest daughter was a student in London. With her friend and their well-earned money from weekend bar work and litter picking in a London park, they bought train tickets to Paris. They had chosen to travel in Europe for their six weeks holiday. Their reinforced nylon back packs stood high above their heads, packed with a lightweight tent, sleeping bag, cooking gear, a couple of books and some scant clothing.

So, I hear you say, not much difference there. Some differences in the funding of our holidays and also the mode of travelling. Lucy moved around by train and local bus. We hitched hiked.

But by far the biggest difference lay in the nature of the trip. We were (in 1966) visiting one country. And were not able or allowed to move to any other country. In 1999 Emily was able to cross back and forth across borders and between nations. She was able to work in beach bars when she ran out of money. When we were near to running out of money, we had to budget to the last lire, and finally use the £5 traveller's cheque my mother had given me for emergencies.

So, what sort of European trip will my granddaughter, now aged fourteen, be able to make when she reaches that magical age of independent travel? It seems to me that if Brexit progresses as promised her summer holiday will look much more like mine rather than her mother's.

PART TWO - THE CONSEQUENCE

The alarm buzzes. The radio switches on automatically.

Today is the first day of the rest of our lives in the United Kingdom. Yes, I mean the non-European, floating alone into the North Sea, United Kingdom. Downstairs I go. So, what's different? The BBC still works. In fact, the Today programme seems rather a jolly affair, with no doom-and-gloom Brexit predictions. They seem to be in "here we are, suck it up" mode. Breakfast... Muesli (Devon), Milk (Welsh), Tea (Kenyan - hmm, I hope they've renegotiated that deal). So today I have two tasks. A visit to the chemist and then a morning's work at the local Foodbank.

As I enter our local pharmacy, I notice a queue winding its way down the aisle as far as the men's toiletries. 'Must be short of staff,' I think to myself. When I eventually get to the counter, I ask politely for my repeat prescription of Thyroxin.

'Sorry, Mrs Arthurs, we have very low stocks, so we would like all our thyroid-deficient customers to return to their GPs and see if a reduced dosage is possible. Thanks. Next please.'

'The Today programme predicted that one,' I thought, and they were spot on.

As I walk towards the Council Offices to start at the Foodbank, I notice a queue of people out in the cold that stretches down the street for fifty yards. This is a small town, and the Foodbank has for some years managed to maintain regular support for those in dire need. But I suspect that this number of needy folk will empty the shelves faster than we can stock them.

'The Today programme didn't predict that one,' I thought.

WRITING HELPS ME TO…

…think outside the box of my life. It allows me a freedom of thought. When we are given a writing task, it sparks something in me which moves and travels in my mind along a sort of creative pathway that has an unpredictability about it. I am never quite sure where it is going, or what the final outcome will look like. This can sometimes be exciting. Sometimes it's funny. Sometimes it can be sad. But it is always immensely satisfying, particularly if I am pleased with what I have written. My husband is a stone sculptor, and, in many ways, the creative process is similar. He is faced with a lump of stone. The final piece is not entirely clear in his mind, but the shape of what he is faced with moves him to change and develop it. It's a creative evolution.

I have always enjoyed writing. It has consistently given me pleasure. When I was spending hours writing reports on observations and assessments of children with difficulties, I enjoyed the process of being able to find the appropriate language and phrases to describe what I had observed, and to make something clear, using accessible, easy to read written language.

I have always enjoyed using written language to persuade and encourage. I think that in my past, in a full-time job, it has been a tool that I have counted on and relied upon. Now my life is different, and I have time to think about writing and why I like it.

I read a tremendous amount and maybe that is what aids my imagination and makes me look more critically at what works for me in terms of a narrative. So, writing helps me focus my mind and concentrate and attempt something that at first, I don't feel capable of doing, but am finally satisfied.

VICKY BALLARD

A CHRISTMAS WISH

The sky darkened menacingly like it did every evening at this time of year, early and mercilessly, without any consideration of the people who worked, or the children who played. The sky informed people it was now time to hurry home; be inside safe or beware.

Franny had unfortunately ignored all the warning signs of the impending storm. She was busy working on her thesis and her mind was in a different world. It was only as the final bells chimed that she realised how late she had let it get. Her skin started prickling; it was Christmas Eve at six p.m. The rules of her country were that she could not be outside from six p.m. onwards. Curfew had been imposed six months previously and, despite all the propaganda informing them of the dire need for them to be home by this time, Franny had ignored it and now she was stuck in a soulless university building, potentially for days.

She ran through the options available to her if she left the building. The catastrophic snowstorm - or the army - could kill her. Neither option really appealed. Her eyes filled up and her stomach started to grumble after hours of being repressed by her studies. Franny was ravenous in a building that likely didn't have even a mince pie. By the glow of her computer she looked around the cold empty room, pulling on her numerous jumpers, hat and gloves that were the staple of every Russian wardrobe.

She started purposefully to go from classroom to classroom, calling out, but all she could hear was her returning echo. She became more and more despondent. She knew that the safest place for her to stay was in the place that she had previously considered her safe haven from the craziness of life outside, but now she was desperate to return to her family and home.

    She leant against a wall and slumped to the floor, gazing at the swirling snow, and trying desperately to see a star. As a child, she used to wish upon them, and her mother had told her that if she believed hard enough, then truly she could do magic. As a child she had truly believed, but as the world grew darker and adulthood harder, she had put aside these childish dreams. Now, for some strange reason, her mother's voice came to her, telling her to believe. Maybe she was just so scared, maybe it was the fear of being alone, but however hard Franny rationalised it, she started to chant, 'I do believe in magic, I do, I do.' She repeated it to herself over and over again until she was barely aware she was doing it, and through the haze she saw her star. 'I wish I were home, I wish I were home,' she chanted, and miraculously Franny was no longer in a cold, empty university, devoid of life, she was in her mother's house, with a stocking at the foot of her bed and the fire warming the whole house. Franny, dazed, ran downstairs to her mother, and her mother just smiled a knowing smile of a woman who had finally finished waiting.

    'Franny, welcome home my love. Finally, you believe.'

THE CHRISTMAS LIST

Dear Santa,

Please, please give me a round-the-world ticket for me and my family. It is so important for me to see my friend, Brooke. I haven't seen her since we lived in Taiwan and I really want my family to meet her family.

    I want my children to see other cultures, and not just live and experience a western way of life. I hope that this experience would make them better world citizens and maybe they will become the catalyst to change the world. So, you see it is very important to give us a round-the-world ticket.

    I would also really like the ticket so that I don't end up living a life of regret for the things I haven't done. I can think of nothing worse than turning round on my death bed lamenting never taking the opportunity to travel.

    So please, please send me these tickets. It would not just fulfil my dreams; it would also fulfil my husband's - so in fact you would be saving on presents!

    Think of this gift as a gift of time for my family. You would be giving us a gift of a year spent together experiencing new things and learning as a family. I appreciate that at four years old, my youngest may not be the best travel companion in remote places, but I think that it would educate them and make them appreciate how lucky they are to have food and toys - in fact, this gift to me would make my children less spoilt, as they wouldn't be able to bring toys with them. Therefore, you would also be helping the plastic problem that is facing the world at the moment.

    If you gave me these tickets, the practicalities of life would be sorted reasonably quickly, so please don't worry about them. The children can come out of school. My husband works on a computer so can work remotely and we can rent out our house. We could possibly do with some travel money, but I don't want to be greedy - so please just send the tickets.

If, on the off chance, you are unable to give me this gift, please be aware that a different sort of gift wouldn't offer the wide range of opportunities that round-the-world tickets offer or affect so many in my family. I would, of course, be grateful for anything and wouldn't like you to think I didn't appreciate your thoughtful gifts, but please remember my house is small and tickets would fit very nicely in my stocking!

I really believe that as you are magical, and the practicalities of travelling around the world in a night doesn't bother you, that you will be able to give this gift to me. Please spread a bit of magic into our lives and make 2019 the best year of our lives.

Forever a believer.

Vicky x

TONY HARDY

Tony Hardy is a self-employed systems engineering consultant who, having recently qualified, is now also working in private practice as an integrative counsellor. He lives in Monmouth and has two teenaged sons.

His hobbies include live music, vegan cookery, running and Portsmouth Football Club. He has always had a keen interest in creative writing, possibly as an antidote to a career spent producing technical reports and specifications. He was previously a member of the Forest of Dean Writers group and contributed to their anthologies of short stories, *Forest – Fact and Fantasy* and *Forest - Fact and Fable*.

A BEGINNING, A MIDDLE AND AN END

Today, it would definitely be opened, come what may, as it had sat inoffensively on the mantelpiece for the last few days. The suspense was now too much not to know, at last, what was written in the bright blue airmail letter.

Jenny took it from the mantelpiece and blew off a cloud of dust. The portrait on the stamp was familiar, she was our Queen too after all, but the legend said Canada and the postmark Vancouver BC. The black, spidery scrawl on the envelope could only be her father's: he'd been taught the 3Rs way back, when that included joined-up handwriting with an ink pen in fear of a well-aimed board rubber from teacher.

Jenny glanced at her husband. John returned a look that said 'good luck' and handed her the letter opener. She carefully slit the envelope from side to side and retrieved four sheets of blue vellum bearing the same black scribble. She cleared her throat and read aloud.

'The greatest advice you can impart to your loved ones on your deathbed is this: don't leave it to your dying breath to gift your life's secrets.'

The silence was broken by the clatter of the letter opener on the slate floor and the splat of a fat, fresh tear.

'By the time you read this I will most likely be gone.'

***

'I'm sorry love,' John comforted his wife.

'Do you mind if I read it to myself, alone?'

'Of course,' he said, 'I'll make some tea,'

Jenny read the letter three times before joining John in the kitchen.

'Well he was a sly old dog,' she eventually said, and as John poured the tea, Jenny poured her heart out.

'So, let's get this straight. He had six children by four different women, so you've got all these half brothers and sisters you never even knew about?'

'Yes. Two over here and four in Canada.'

'And the houses?'

'One over here, Railway Cottage, that's been empty for years. He's left it to me in his will.'

'Wow!'

'And one in Canada.'

'Yes. To be sold and shared between the other children.'

'And do you think you'll want to meet all your new family?'

'Don't know. A trip to Vancouver might be nice. But first we need to sort out the house here'

***

And so it was that John and Jenny found themselves at Railway Cottage that April morning. It was the end cottage in a terrace originally built for the workers on the Wye Valley line, now long gone. Being the end of terrace, it had a larger garden than the other cottages, but that was not the blessing it might have seemed, given the amount of work it was going to take to clear the growth of weeds and restore it to its past glory. But they were here to sort out the inside of Railway Cottage today. Jenny opened the front door and pushed aside the mountain of junk mail. Spiders and beetles scurried across the hallway like her father's handwriting. The house smelled of damp and emptiness. Beneath the dust and cobwebs, it was straight out of one of those documentaries about how we lived in the Fifties.

'It must have been empty for years,' Jenny said.

'This is going to be quite some job. Are you sure you're OK to do this?'

'Yes,' she said, 'Let's get on with it.'

***

At long last they'd finished clearing the old man's house: unravelling eighty years of secrets, finding the answers to some questions, opening up a whole host more. It had been a tough task, taking them through every emotion, from the joy of the fondest memories to despair at some of the cruel things he'd done, even if he had been good intentioned. All the while, they felt he was up there, looking down on them, guiding them, holding their hands.

    Jenny left first and sat waiting in the car for John. A final glance around the room, checking all was in order, lights all off, and he stepped out into the twilight, and glanced up to the perfect crescent moon.

ABOVE LLANTHONY PRIORY

My friends call me a curmudgeon and it's a suit that fits me well. I prefer winter to summer, darkness to light. I'm not a gregarious soul, solitude is more my thing. I'm not one for pushing out the boat, for hosting lavish parties. Where others revel in excess, I see the flip side of that coin: deprivation and suffering, misery and want. Praise sits uncomfortably with me. I always feel others are far more deserving. Happiness is mostly an unwelcome visitor, encroaching, intruding, bringing with it guilt at others' misfortune.

But today is the first day of spring. My boots go on at first light. Not expensive, new Gore-Tex, but well-worn Italian leather, its life expectancy lengthened by regular application of dubbin. The soles and laces have been replaced so often, my boots have a feel of Trigger's broom to them. I carry a staff of beech to help steady me on the rocky path. A simple packed lunch to provide sustenance, and a flask of hot tea. These are my companions for the day.

I make the slow steady climb out of Pandy and onto Hatherall Hill. The early morning sun is warm on my skin, causing steam to rise from my arms and face into the chill air. I gasp for breath until I get into my stride then I am like a mountain goat, clambering over rocks, effortlessly gaining altitude until I am finally on that magnificent ridge. The crest undulates like the backbone of a giant green whale. To my right is England, the land of my birth. To my left is Wales, my adopted home. Ahead of me, the trail well-trodden by many before me, and by myself oftentimes. Hawks soar above me, sheep scatter at the landing of my feet. Rabbits dart about, through the short grass and purple heather, swallowed up by the subterranean warrens they have carved for themselves. Below in the valley, life proceeds at a sedentary pace. A tractor here, a car there, sun reflecting off the occasional farmhouse window.

Ahead of me I see my destination. Just a triangulation point, but it represents the spot where the path comes down off the ridge towards Llanthony Priory, my special place. Where the monastic ruins blend into the lush green pastures of the Vale of Ewyas, the Black Mountains providing a dramatic backdrop for a pint in the higgledy-piggledy hotchpotch hotel. Before I make my descent, I stop and pour myself a mug of tea and sit and take in the breath-taking views that unfold all around me. Such modest happiness I think I can bear.

A BOX OF MEMORIES

Thomas sat on an upturned packing crate in the cold, unfurnished room. Outside, a howling northerly tossed leaves around and threw twigs and branches at the full-length windows. His garden, like most of the house, was empty, but the light and warmth of the neighbours' gardens spilled into his. Festive lights twinkled and the swirling wind intermittently brought carol singing into earshot.

Thomas ripped open a large cardboard box marked 'Photos – Assorted' to reveal a bank of blue photo albums. He thought to himself that the contents of this box, and there must have been around forty albums inside, would fit on the tiniest storage card on one of the mobile phones that everyone had in today's instant and throwaway world. But that wasn't for him. He loved the feel of a photo album. The wrinkled leather covers. The shiny cellophane covering page upon page of reminiscence. The sturdiness of the album's spine. He adored the smell of them, part musty and part new, plastic and dust. And he loved the sound they made as he flicked his way down memory lane, the leather bindings creaking, the pages thudding against each other.

The first album he pulled out of the box was labelled 'Winter 1974.' He remembered it so well. The snowman he and his brother had made in the garden. The days off school, tobogganing down the big hill in Leigh Park Gardens. The time he broke his wrist ice skating on the school playground. They were so young and carefree then. The world lay at their feet.

He put the first album down and picked up a second 'Christmas 1996.' These memories belonged to the adult Thomas. A Thomas who had a wife. A Thomas who'd got out and explored some of that world that once lay at his feet.

Christmas 1996 was spent, not knee deep in snow, but on a sunny beach in Melbourne. There were photos of him swimming in the sea, and cooking on a barbecue. Photos of his wife sunbathing. Long, uninterrupted stretches of sand and surf.

Now here he was again. Winter 2018. No wife, no sunshine. No photos. Just an empty house, braced against the bitter cold.

AUSTERITY

It's for the good of the nation, they say
We must live within our means.
Tell that to a mother trying to feed
Three kids on a tin of beans.

How are we going to make ends meet?
Dad's not worked for years.
Payday loans and Foodbanks
Mum's reduced to tears.

Pensioners forced to choose between
Gas bills or shoes on feet.
City centres like refugee camps
Tents on every street.

No dustbin men, no teachers
No jobs, no libraries, no buses.
No end to hospital waiting lists
No consultants, no doctors, no nurses.

Suicide rates the highest
in decades, every cut they make
Slashes the heart of the nation
A nation that's at break-

-ing point, when will it end?
How much worse can things get
They say Austerity is the only way?
Yet the country's more in debt.

And those who run the country,
Those whose banks are full
Get rich, fat cats get fatter
As they speculate and gamble

Not with pounds shillings and pence
But with people's hearts, souls, and minds.
Austerity is murder, ideologically driven
Not being cruel to be kind.

BEANZ MEANZ HEINZ

PART ONE – FROM THE OUTSIDE

'Four hundred and sixty-five,' said Moby, with a confidence that belied his lowly status as the youngest of the three brothers. Short and scrawny, bespectacled and with a shock of bright red hair, he had gained the nickname Moby because the others thought he was a "bit of a dick." But he was adamant.

'Four hundred and sixty-five.' he repeated.

'There's never that many,' said Terry, the oldest of the three. Aged twelve, Terry was starting to fill out a bit and towered over the other two, both physically and in terms of family pecking order. 'Two hundred, tops.'

'Give me that!' Gary, the middle brother, interrupted and grabbed the can. Gary was neither scrawny nor tall, fat nor thin. Just an average ten-year-old boy. Imagining it might help in some way, he shook the can and held it to his ear.

'You're both wrong,' he announced. 'Five hundred and seventy-seven.'

He threw the can as high above his head as he could. The others tumbled out of the way as it came back down, but Gary pouched it with a catch a slip fielder would have been proud of.

'So how are we going to settle this?' he asked.

'I know,' chimed Moby, 'let's ask a grown-up, they know everything.'

Terry laughed. 'They don't know everything, and besides, all the grown-ups will be at work now.'

'It must say somewhere on the can,' said Gary. He held the can in front of his face and started to read. 'HEINZ BEANZ in tomato sauce... da-di-da-di-da.... dum-di-dum-di-dum... what's mono... sodium.... glue...ta...mate?'

'Dunno,' said Terry.

'Nope,' Gary continued, 'nothing on here that says how many.'

'We're gonna have to open it and count 'em,' said Moby.

'Well how are we gonna do that?' asked Terry.

'Dad's got an axe in the shed!' said Moby.

'Yeah right, we'd smash it to pieces and probably cut our hands off too,' said Terry.

'And then Dad would kill us,' Gary added. 'We need one of those things. You know. I've seen Mum use them. They're made of metal. She sticks them into cans and then twists like a handle thingy and the can is opened.'

'Yeah we could do that,' said Moby.

'We don't know how to use one,' said Gary.

'We'll work it out, I'm sure.' Terry was now the confident one. 'Last one to the kitchen is a big girl.'

They raced across the fields back towards their house on the edge of the estate. Terry in front, his long legs carrying him faster than the other two. Gary in the middle, clutching onto the tin for dear life. Moby at the back, zigzagging around, arms outstretched, pretending to be a Spitfire. 'Daga-daga-daga-daga-daga. Take that Jerry.'

Terry was first home and opened the gate. Moby, fresh from defeating the Luftwaffe, darted in ahead of Gary, leaving his brother to assume the status of big girl. Terry opened the kitchen door, and the three brothers began rifling through the kitchen drawers.

'Is this it?' asked Moby excitedly.

'No, you moron, that's a tea strainer. This is it.' Terry held up the shining metal contraption with a look of wonderment. 'But what do we do with it?'

'I think it's like this,' said Gary. He punctured the bottom of the upside-down tin and started twisting the handle. Within seconds there was tomato sauce and jagged metal everywhere, but he had achieved his objective. He poured the cold beans into a bowl and set the empty can on the worktop, right way up.

'Here, what's this?' asked Moby, picking at the can's ring-pull.

'Idiot!' said Terry.

'Right, let's get counting.'

Transferring a bean at a time from the bowl back into the can, the boys slowly began to count. 'One, two, three, four, ….'

Terry looked crestfallen as the can was barely half full when the count ticked over from one-hundred and ninety-nine to two hundred. Gary didn't seem too optimistic either. Moby had a knowingly smug look on his face. The tension mounted as they got into the three hundreds then the four hundreds. None of them heard the kitchen door open at four hundred and fifty-two.

'Four hundred and sixty-three, four hundred and sixty-four.' Terry picked the last bean out of the bowl.

'I don't believe it. Four hundred and sixty-five. The jammy so-and-so got it absolutely spot on.'

Moby leapt up, ready to take on more Messerschmidt pilots, but as he took off into the skies above the English Channel he ran straight into his mother's midriff.

'What the hell has been going on in here?'

PART TWO – ON THE INSIDE

Archibald Bean let out a blood-curdling scream as he fell from the boy's hand into the bowl and made a dull 'plup' sound as he landed in the cold tomato sauce. Two feet is one helluva long drop when you're a baked bean and have never ventured outside the can before.

'Hello, old bean,' he said to his friend Cuthbert Bean, who he was now lying next to in the sauce. 'Fancy meeting you here.'

'Fancy, indeed,' said Cuthbert. 'Do you have any idea what's going on?'

'Not really,' replied Archibald. 'When I signed up for this, the job description said we would just sit in the dark for a few days or weeks, until one day we'd be poured into a saucepan and get boiled to death. None of this counting nonsense or being man-handled by horrid little children.'

'No, it's not right,' Cuthbert agreed.

The two beans had known each other since they had been young haricot beans together in the field in Idaho. They had been harvested, packaged, and shipped out at the same time, and against all odds, had ended up in the same can. They could have passed for brothers. They had the same oval shape, the same garish, orange glow and identical markings on their husks. Archibald was a day older than Cuthbert, but Cuthbert was ever so slightly larger.

'Have you spoken to any of the others?' asked Cuthbert.

'Not really,' Archibald replied, 'there's four hundred and sixty-three of them and I wouldn't know where to start.'

'I was chatting to twins from Michigan. They'd never known anything like this either. I think we're all at a bit of a loss.'

'Most peculiar behaviour,' Archibald continued. "I'd heard humans were strange, but I never thought they would be weird enough to count baked beans in a can.'

'Imagine if we counted the humans at the dinner table.' Cuthbert laughed a very beany laugh.

'Imagine.'

Cuthbert was first to notice the commotion across the sea of beans and sauce. Some of the beans were pointing their little beany arms into the air and screaming little beany screams. Archibald noticed a giant human hand reach out and pick up the bowl.

'Oh no. It's not...' he said.

'Oh Jesus, please no. What a way to go.' The fear in Cuthbert's voice was audible above the general bean hubbub.

Mrs Brown turned the dial and grinned a very satisfied grin as she waited patiently. They were doing very well for themselves, thank you very much, and she was the proudest woman on Marigold Close when she'd taken delivery of one of those new-fangled microwave ovens. The whirling of the oven drowned out the sound of four hundred and sixty-five screaming baked beans whose lives ended with a deafening 'PING.'

CHRISTMAS – DARK AND LIGHT

PART ONE – DARK

Dear Clarice

As the nights lengthen and Christmas draws ever nearer, the city braces itself for the annual onslaught of unbridled consumerism and drunken debauchery.

Edinburgh, of all places, attracts the hordes. By day, Princes Street seduces shoppers into parting with their hard-earned cash in exchange for gifts for their loved ones. By night, the bars of the Royal Mile welcome myriad revellers, fill them with seasonal cheer and spew them back out onto the streets.

But this season, Edinburgh may have my body, but it won't have my spirit. No loved one for me to buy presents for, no tree under which to place festive gifts. No tinsel or fairy lights decorate my barren apartment, a miserable testimony to my loneliness. Not for me the camaraderie of an office party in one of those swanky bars, or a kiss stolen under the mistletoe. Just solitude and pain, envy, and grief. An imaginary advent calendar counting down to the second of January, when it will all be over.

And why? Because of you Clarice, because of you. Because you chose him over me. Because you chose his arms to run into, not mine. Because you saw his future as your future, leaving what we had together well and truly in your past.

Red is the colour of Christmas. Santa's coat, Rudolph's nose. Claret with the roast turkey. A carrot on a snowman's face. Red is the colour of my Christmas too. It's the shade my eyes turn, as I cry myself to sleep at night. It's the rage I feel in my heart and the fire of resentment burning in my belly.

Red is the colour of the blood that will flow out of my wrists when I finally escape this season of misery. Blood that will be on your hands.

PART TWO – LIGHT

Dear Clarice

The Christmas lights were put on in the city on Saturday and, as ever, it was a truly joyous sight. I love Edinburgh at this time of year, there's really no better place to be. On Princes Street the festive shoppers are torn between going into the stores to pick up gifts for their loved ones, and simply standing in the street looking up with amazement at the dazzling displays above them. Along the Royal Mile, revellers spill out of the pubs and bars, their faces ruby red from over-indulging in Christmas spirits, and their eyes lit up, twinkling along with the backdrop of sparkling lights. Lovers, colleagues, or maybe just acquaintances, steal furtive kisses under the mistletoe. Partygoers belt out seasonal tunes: Last Christmas, White Christmas, and I Wish It Could be Christmas Every Day.

It was such a wonderful feeling, that I simply had to run home and dress the tree and fill my apartment with decorations. I am so looking forward to Christmas this year, and my excitement builds with every door I open on the advent calendar. What a contrast to last Christmas, which was such a miserable one for me.

And why? Because of you Clarice, because of you. Because you chose me over him. Because you chose my arms to run into, not his. Because you saw a future with us together, not apart. Each advent chocolate means I am one day nearer to seeing you again. Each bauble on the tree makes me think of all the Christmases I will spend with you. Each gift under the tree has been chosen with all my love.

Merry Christmas, darling.

DEAD TOWN

Eighteen years old and rightfully dying to get out of this place.

This one-horse town, this dead-end street,

Where folks are born to grow old, wither and die

With nothing to punctuate their story, barely a heartbeat.

But not me I've got the world at my feet.

Gonna find me a girl, gonna buy me a car.

Gonna hit the open road, scream past my old school

Where they suck the life out of you, make you into one of them.

Keep your head down, play by the rules.

But not me, I'm nobody's fool

Past the town's only factory, where they take in

Human beings, metals, plastics, rubber, alike.

Process them all the same, churn out automobiles, pollution,

And empty husks of people, I'm gonna take a hike.

I'm outta here man, I'm on my bike

The highway's there before me, stretching out

across the desert, over mountains, into outer space.

This road is taking me to my life, to my dreams.

A melting pot of cultures, of exotic sounds, exquisite tastes.

It's mine to conquer, to feel, to see, no time to waste.

Only got one life, gonna live my life to the full.

Gonna make me some memories to last for ever.

Gonna meet crazy people, heroes, ordinary folks.

Laugh until I cry, dance like I never

Danced before, go at it hell for leather.

And when I've been around the world, gonna head back to my home.

Gonna come back with a truck, a bus, a Greyhound.

Fill it with folks no matter how old and rightfully dying to get out of that place.

Gonna get them to break out of their chains, thrown their tools down.

Gonna get them to leave that old dead town.

EULOGY

When death comes, we celebrate life. However ordinary, however brief. However remarkable or enduring. All lives lived are worthy of our kindest words.

Samira Midari lived the briefest of lives. Her life wasn't long enough to be considered ordinary or anything else. But her story is remarkable. Her parents lived in Aleppo, in northern Syria. Their neighbourhood was shelled on a daily basis. Her father Khaled made his way through the rubble every day to open up the family shop, until that too was bombed, and their livelihood destroyed. Desperate and scared, they took what they could carry in a single suitcase and fled the city. Unbeknown to Khaled, his wife Noura was carrying their most precious belonging: she was newly pregnant with Samira.

They joined the column of human ants fleeing the wreckage of a once great city. No idea really where they were going, just following like sheep. After two weeks of walking along cratered roads, exposed to the heat of the days and the cold of the nights, they reached a refugee camp near the Turkish border. Here they received shelter and minimal food, and here, seeing her sick every morning, Khaled realised that Noura was pregnant, and made the fateful decision to escape the camp and head for the Mediterranean Sea. She was, in fact, six months pregnant by this time, and eight months gone by the time they had got out of the camp and made it to within a mile of the border. Baby Samira knew nothing of the world she was coming in to. She decided to arrive a month early, and so it was in a makeshift shelter beside a bomb-cratered highway, that she was born.

That same day, a sortie of Russian fighter planes flew over and strafed a convoy of military trucks making its way south. Several trucks were destroyed, and dozens of soldiers killed. The Midari family's shelter was caught in the crossfire. Samira and her father were killed instantly. Noura was badly wounded but survived. To this day she wishes she hadn't.

Samira Midari was just a few hours old. She was beautiful. She was innocent. She was loved. Today we mourn Samira and celebrate that she was all of those things. Today we mourn the death of a nation. We mourn the decimated generation of a proud race. We mourn the passing of civilisation into savagery. We mourn all those lost in futile, deathly conflict. We mourn all those who are statistics of governments and playthings of warlords.

We mourn Samira, may she rest in peace, and may we one day celebrate that her death wasn't in vain. We celebrate her mother's strength and dignity and her remarkable story. We welcome her into our community and hope that she can rebuild her life.

FIRST DAY OF SPRING

It was one of life's crueller ironies. The first day of spring was the last day of his mother's life. A time when most of us are full of hope, of anticipation, surrounded by new life, was the time when she arrived at her final full stop.

The year she died, he barely noticed the passing of spring. Her illness coincided with the three months of winter, but whenever it had come, the days would have run one into another, dark, tormented, caged in that airless hospital room. Rarely venturing outside. Sat day after day by her bedside, weighed down with the knowledge of the unshakable and the inevitable. Even when the end came, he was consumed by funeral arrangements, and disposing of her estate, and overcome with such deep, overwhelming grief that it was nearly winter again before he came up for breath.

The first anniversary of her passing was just as hard. Reminders as the day approached. Thoughts back to those unbearable nights on the cancer ward. Memories of his mother full of tubes and drugs, being poked and probed by a never-ending procession of medical staff. Him not knowing what to do with himself, helpless against this evil disease, barely eating or sleeping, barely functioning. One year on, everyone around was getting on with their lives, waking up with spring, unwinding, uncovering, undying. Him stuck in time, as dead as his poor mother, yet somehow living.

But they say time is a great healer. This time of year had got easier for him. It wasn't just a case of time passing, pain lifting, sad memories of her difficult end slowly being replaced by a lifetime of happy flashbacks from a life lived and enjoyed to the full. Three years ago he made a conscious decision to make the spring equinox a celebration of her life and the beginning of a new adventure, each year vowing to do something different, something that would make his mother proud, make her laugh, make her cry, something she'd want to tell all her friends about. This year was no different.

He was up at first light with a small bunch of white lilies, which he took with him to the pebbled beach, just to the west of the main pier. It was here her ashes had been scattered on the first anniversary of her passing. In hindsight that had been the start of the healing process, as the early spring breeze on the day had not taken her off into the sea as planned but had deposited her in a thin film all over him and his brother. It was the first time both of them had laughed in eighteen months, and once they started laughing, they didn't stop until they'd hugged out each other's tears. The thoughts of that day came back to him vividly as he said a few words to mum and tossed the lilies into the sea – no breeze today.

He then made the short walk back to his B&B and got changed out of his warm clothes. The sun was up now, and the early mist had burned away to give rise to one of those perfect spring mornings. Warm, not hot, clear blue skies, no wind. Perfect. He slipped on his shorts and laced up his running shoes. Last on was his vest. On the front were his race number and the Cancer Charity logo, on the back was written 'For Mum.' He made the short walk along the promenade to the start line and joined the thousands of other runners in nervous but excited anticipation.

Five hours and seventeen minutes later, there were tears in his eyes again. This time tears of joy, of pride, of achievement. He'd been through every emotion today – pain, elation, exhaustion, wanting to give up, refusing to give up. He'd given blood, sweat and tears for twenty-six miles and every part of his body was aching, but he'd done it.

So now it was dusk on the first day of spring. He'd celebrated his mother's life and done something that both he and she could be immensely proud of and, as the sun set, he kissed his medal and raised a glass of mum's favourite cabernet sauvignon in her memory.

GUY FAWKES NIGHT

I sat on a crooked stool in a corner of the tavern. Although the place was a cacophony of sound – market traders haggled, a jester entertained a small crowd, and three ladies of ill-repute laid temptation before a group of travelling salesmen – I hadn't spoken for what seemed like an age. My companion, desperate for a reaction, took a sip of his mead and banged his tankard on the table.

'I wish you hadn't told me,' I said.

'I had to tell someone,' said Guy, 'it was tearing me up inside.'

'And you're serious; you're going through with it?'

'Deadly serious.'

'And deadly is the word,' I said. I picked up my drink and took a large gulp. 'When?' I asked.

'Tonight's the night,' said Guy, 'are you in or out?'

'Drink up,' I said, 'let's walk and talk. Too many earwiggers and blabbermouths in here.' We both downed our ales, and I banged some small coins down onto the table.

'Thank you, Nellie,' I said as we left.

Outside, the November air was cold and biting in stark contrast to the hot, thick atmosphere of the tavern. We walked along the lane that skirted the marketplace and led down to the Thames. The market was in full cry. Traders waxed lyrical about their wares. Animals bleated and grunted as they were shoved into holding pens. A dispute between a shepherd and a moneylender was threatening to boil over into a full-scale punch-up.

'The explosives are in place,' Guy said, 'I'll be going down into the tunnels to set them off as soon as their Lordships are in the Palace. I've got comrades keeping watch at all the strategic points.'

'So, where do I fit in the plan?' I asked.

'Well, I need someone to help us make good our escape. You've got an ass and a cart, haven't you?'

'I have. But I'm not sure I want to get involved. They'll hang the lot of you and have your heads on spikes outside the Tower if you get caught.'

'You think I don't know that? And anyway, you're already involved, just by talking to me. Once this lot goes up, they'll be bringing in all known acquaintances for questioning and I don't think they'll care much for the truth.'

'That's about right. And don't think I don't believe in the cause. Those Lords have had it coming to them for a long time. Things can't go on like this, the time is right for change.'

'That's the spirit,' said Guy, 'and if we pull this off, we'll go down in history.'

'Imagine that,' I said, 'hey, maybe they'll call a national day of celebration, and name it after us?'

'You never know,' said Guy and he shook my hand.

'That's settled then,' he said, 'it's all going off at midnight. Meet me on the corner of Parliament Square, with your carriage.'

Not sure of what I'd just agreed to, I went off to prepare my animal for its fateful night.

He could hear the tunnels filling with the footsteps of the King's men. No time to prime the powder. No time to set the fuse, just run. Get the hell out of there, and hope that his man was waiting in the getaway cart. He dropped everything and sprinted along the dark, echoing tunnel, too afraid to look back over his shoulder. At the end of the tunnel, he hauled himself up the rope that he knew would bring him out onto Parliament Square. Carefully lifting the drain cover, he peered into the darkness to check the coast was clear. There he saw the carriage waiting for him, just like they planned. He pulled himself into the cold London night and darted across the square, flinging himself into the back of the cart.

'We need to get out of here. As quick as you can!'

'I don't think so Fawkes.' The arresting officer turned from the driver's seat to face him, cocking his pistol with a loud snap that said the game was up. 'The only place you're going is the Tower.' Within seconds the cart was surrounded by the King's soldiers, and Guy Fawkes was being led away, a loaded gun to his head.

I awoke in a strange bed in an unfamiliar part of London. I could hear an unholy commotion going on outside.

'Oyez, oyez, oyez.' A single bell rang out.

'Oyez. Gunpowder plot foiled. King's life saved.'

'Oyez. Traitor sent to the Tower.'

And then all that could be heard was eager chatter, as the townsfolk took in what they'd heard, and discussed what they knew about the plot. Rumours of this, accounts of that. I tried to take it all in, but my thoughts were interrupted by a knock on the door. My heart leapt, but then I remembered where I was. Not on the run, but safe. In a safe house.

'Your breakfast sir.'

I thanked the maid but left the food untouched on the bedside table. I was hungry, but I couldn't face it. Sick with treachery. Unable to eat because of my betrayal. Knowing the fate that awaited my old friend Guido.

HOME

I have never wanted to be alone

But here I stand

Alone in a crowd

Of scornful faces that hate,

Of people who don't know me

But think they can read my sun-baked skin.

I am a book judged by its cover.

'Paki, go home,' they say, ignorant.

I have never wanted to be alone.

I crave to be the heart

Of family, of community,

Of a proud people.

But hope is ripped apart.

Torn down brick by brick.

By bombs and by guns,

By rape and by gas.

I have never wanted to be alone.

Safety in numbers, they say.

Clinging to a decrepit dinghy,

Battered by an unforgiving sea.

Crammed like cattle in the back of a truck.

Abandoned in a foreign land.

Please don't leave me,

Not here, alone.

I have never wanted to be alone.

Mother, drowned.

Father, shot.

Brother betrayed and tortured.

Sister detained and deported.

So here I am alone.

So far from home.

And so very, very alone.

HOUSE OF FOOLS

Who will come to put out the fires,
Reconcile the fiercest of foes?
Patch up the broken and wounded,
Staunch the bloodiest nose?

Who will pick up the pieces
Of bridges broken, their stones
Stolen, and used to build walls
Round a castle, an Englishman's home?

Who will rebuild a future
For the young and the weak and the frail?
Those whose voices were drowned out by the fools,
Those who weren't given a say.

Who will hold the fools to account
For playing Russian roulette with our fate?
Ideological insanity.
Extramarital affairs of the state.

Who will give us a second chance?

Who will forgive and forget?

Will we learn, or is it too late?

Or maybe there's hope for us yet.

IN TIMES OF COVID

PART ONE - ON THE OUTSIDE

I press my nose to the cold windowpane, and it steams up immediately. I wipe away the mist with the sleeve of my shirt, worried that I will miss something. But there is nothing. No people. No cars. No sound. Normally this would be a busy thoroughfare. The revving of engines and the slamming of car doors, as schoolchildren are deposited for the day. The hum of traffic impatiently queuing for parking spaces in the town, their occupants eager to do a day's work. Children laughing and chatting. Old women stopping to gossip. Dog walkers barking commands at their beloved pets. But there is none of that today. Neither has there been any of that for the past... oh I forget how long. It seems like this bizarre situation has been with us forever now. In the near silence, each sound is amplified. In the emptiness, all presence is exaggerated. In the stillness, every movement is tectonic. A grey sky weighs down on the town as if to squeeze us into our homes, imprison us for another day.

The bell in the school clock tower strikes nine times, each peel echoing out and rolling down the empty street. The publican across the road opens an upstairs window and the creaking of its rusty hinges weaves between the bell's notes. A police siren adds to the cacophony before disappearing onto the empty dual carriageway towards Ross. Beyond the grey tarmac, the river can be heard, bubbling its way towards the Bristol Channel. Before these times it was easy to forget the river was even there, such was the multitude of distractions obscuring it from sight and sound. Now I can see the water glisten in the early morning sun; hear herons and kingfishers calling on the water. The river seems to have regained its lost place at the heart of the community.

    A lone runner jogs past, his heavy footsteps like a solitary, metronomic drummer. Normally they roam in packs, an army of sweating and panting, and out of breath conversation. Normally I would be one of them. Today I just look on wistfully as he plods by, and I take a step back from the window.

PART TWO - ON THE INSIDE

As I retreat, I feel both the comfort of my safe space and the confines of my prison. I have come to know these four walls so well over the previous few months. Although I have been staring through a glass pane for the past fifteen minutes, the true window to the world is now the laptop on my desk. It delivers news and entertainment. It enables human contact via the miracle of Zoom. It allows me to earn a living, in a new kind of workplace where nobody sees you below the waist. But for all the good this electronic portal has been during lockdown, it is no substitute for the real world. The news website doesn't rustle or smell like a broadsheet. There are no random water cooler chats on Zoom. You cannot hug moving pixels.

    I have come to know my kitchen way better than is healthy. So much time on my hands for creating new culinary masterpieces. So little discipline when it comes to eating them. So many inches added to the waistline. Beyond the kitchen door, my shed has been a major beneficiary of lockdown, its corrugated Perspex roof and striking white guttering a proud testament to my newfound DIY skills.

    Upstairs, my bedroom is a conundrum. A reminder of my solitude, but a haven from the madness outside. A place where I rest and recharge, but a reminder that I have no meaningful exertions to rest and recharge from. A place where it would be so easy to spend days on end, with nothing to get up for, but a place I know I need to leave with routine regularity lest I descend into a cesspool of idleness, wallowing and despair. The boys' bedrooms are contrasting reminders to me: one lies empty with the eldest son quarantined elsewhere; the other contains a deliriously happy teenager, with no school to go to, oblivious to the pandemic in his PlayStation isolation.

I have walked between these rooms so many times during the past few months. Footprints that should have been left in the outside world, evidence of good times, new discoveries, wild adventures, instead have worn permanent pathways in this miniature, unreal realm.

PART THREE - A TIME OF CHANGE

The year feels like it has been played in reverse. Spring, the time of new beginnings, was when we started to shut down. We retreated into indoor worlds. We spurned human contact. We turned inwards. We died a little. Now it is autumn, a time when nature would be readying itself for a harsh winter by shedding leaves, hoarding food, filling the rivers. Instead we are seeing the first green shoots of recovery starting to appear. We are tentatively venturing outside, first in our two-household bubbles, then in our socially distanced groups. We've put on our masks and we've eaten out to help out. We are slowly returning to normal, even if it's not the normal we thought was normal before everything became so abnormal.

    I am staring out of the window less and opening the front door more. Traffic noise is beginning to return. Children are back in school, with all the noise and activity that brings to my street. The pub is open again, and the noise that brings is both welcome – when I'm part of it – and unwelcome, when its source is unruly teenagers disrespecting social distancing rules and keeping me awake at night. There is more pedestrian traffic outside my house, and I can hear the comforting chatter of passers-by once again.

    Inside, the house is slowly changing. There are shoes on the doormat now, and those shoes are dirty more often than they have been recently. Coats and jackets on their hooks have a recently-worn look, rather than resembling museum artefacts, gathering dust, and freeze-framing time. There have been visitors, and there is evidence of those visitors. Solitary cups on the draining board have been replaced by social gatherings of crockery. The sofa has remnant indentations from human backsides, and there may be one or two empty wine bottles going out for recycling.

The changes are tentative, because we know our new freedoms can be taken away at any minute, should we take a step too far back into the old normal. For now, we are content with a "new, new normal" which lies somewhere between the old normal and the new normal. A normal where we stay "in" but venture "out"; where we isolate socially or socialise in isolation; where we reach out for what we desperately crave but cherish dearly what we have.

We humans are resilient types. They say what doesn't kill us makes us stronger. It's just as well in these unprecedented times.

LANTERN PARADE

It's the first Friday in December and a large crowd has gathered by the historic Monnow Bridge. It's a cold, crisp evening and the River Monnow glistens below the bridge, reflecting the full moon and the town's Christmas lights. The buzz of excitement fills the night air. Gaily coloured hats and scarves, big coats, collars turned up or hoods pulled on, and warm gloves are the order of the day. Some seek heat in the Gatehouse pub and the chip shop next door while they wait for the parade to start. Volunteers hand out lanterns to the revellers of Monmouth. Not, as in years gone by, real candles for the candlelit parade, but flickering LED tea lights – health and safety gone mad. The crowd is young and old. Excited children with exasperated parents, wondering when it will all start, and they can let the kids off the leash. Elderly residents of the town, keeping the tradition alive. Newcomers, keen to take part in their first parade. Exiles, returning to visit their hometown on this special night.

At just before six o'clock, the crowd falls quiet as the Mayor takes the stage. He clears his throat then proceeds to thank the sponsors and welcome everyone to this year's parade. Then the brass band strikes up "Hark the Herald Angels" and the townsfolk fall in behind the band, forming a slow procession up Monnow Street, singing cheerily along to the carol.

The street is closed to traffic, and excited children dart from side to side, weaving through the procession, squealing with excitement. Traders line the street, selling sweets and glow sticks, hot dogs, and gluhwein. The smell of the food and drink says Christmas as much as the sights and sounds do. Adults in the parade hold up their flickering lanterns, sing along to the carols and exchange stories and laughs with their friends. Those who haven't joined the parade watch from the sidelines and wave from the doorways of pubs, as they take on board their Christmas cheer.

Monnow Street is only short – wide in the middle and narrow at the ends, a hangover from mediaeval times when the pinch points were used to stop cattle escaping the town's markets - but the walk up the hill to Agincourt Square takes a good twenty minutes, and four or five carols. The Mayor calls the procession to a halt and says a few more words of thanks. He encourages the townsfolk to spend their money at the stalls or put it in the charity buckets. The crowd disperses and the band strikes up again. In the square there are more food and drink vendors, and a number of craft stalls selling festive gifts. The crowd now line the street to await the arrival of the main man. The children know who it's going to be, and they are at fever pitch. After a short while the band stops playing and a voice cries 'here he comes.'

The sound of sleigh bells is soon heard, and the air is filled with cries and shrieks as Santa pulls up in the square. Henry V and Charles Rolls look down with interest. Santa retrieves his sack from the sleigh and makes his way through the crowds into his grotto, deep within the bowels of the Shire Hall. Children pour into the hall in eager anticipation. Adults dissipate into the pubs of Monmouth and mark the official start of Monmouth's Christmas with a few warming drinks.

Now I know it's nearly Christmas.

MOTHER'S DAY

The sun shone down that day.

Its warmth made us screw up our eyes.

Cracking our lamprey mouths into broad smiles.

But it was she who really made us smile.

We remembered how she cared for us all.

Like a mother duck rounding up her yellow balls of tumbleweed

Before shooing them across the road.

How she would captivate every room, flitting between us

Like a butterfly visits every nectar-laden flower in nature's garden.

How she gave the milk of human kindness

To her suckling litter, then when the time was right,

Set us free, like a mother swallow, whose fledglings take first flight.

How even when we had flown,

She watched us like a hawk. She knew each

and every one of us - what made us happy, what made us fright.

How she was bright like fireflies.

Had the wisdom of an owl, the cunning of a fox,

The laughter of a hyena, and yet the strength of an ox.

How she always had the right word,

A plaster for every scratch, a potion for every ill.

How she kept her gaggle of geese together through rain and shine.

And now at last she's made us cry.

Tears of sadness that mother hen has left.

Tears of joy that we had her for our mother at all.

The sun shone down that day

When we committed her body to the ground

Where her warmth spread into the welcoming earth.

NEVADA TRILOGY

PART ONE - NEVADA BLACKTOP

The open road stretched out for miles. Tarmac baked in the desert sun. Heat haze made its surface shimmer like a black river, straight as an arrow, shooting off to the distant mountain ranges. The highway, hemmed in by unnecessary yellow lines, was striped with light and dark bands of molten rubber. A dashed line down the centre, kept city bound traffic apart from traffic heading into the wilderness.

    Unfolding either side of the road, a blood red moonscape of burning sand was littered with barren rocks and darting tumbleweed. Cactus plants stood proud, marshalled by hardy lizards. Wind licked at the rocks and carried off into the distance the chirping of cicadas and rattling of snakes.

    Above the desert, wispy strands of pure white cloud, flecked across the deepest of blue skies, turning the scene into a natural tricolour. Stratospheric winds gathered up tendrils of cloud to form a surreal, giant white vulture, poised to swoop for carrion.

    The empty freeway was an open book, waiting for an adventure to be written.

PART TWO - CAR WASH

His feet ached from standing all day. His back cricked and strained from carrying pail upon pail of water, from stretching to reach his cloth into the furthest corners. His hands were blistered from being in water all day, and his throat was parched from hard graft.

He was a tall man, six foot two in the heeled leather boots he wore over his ripped denim jeans, but that made his job easier. He wore a brown leather belt, which held in place the plain white vest that showcased his muscular definition and dark tan. He wore his jet-black hair in a ponytail under a blue baseball cap, which sat back to front to protect his neck from the fierce sun. His eyes were hidden by designer shades, but folks told him they were the kind of eyes you could lose yourself in.

His face was a field of stubble, sun-baked from working outside. It looked almost statuesque, chiselled from stone, until it cracked with pride at the job he'd finished.

The row of cars glistened on the showroom forecourt, ready to seduce helpless customers. His day's work was done.

PART THREE - ACTING ON IMPULSE

He didn't know what had come over him. The seductive glistening of the newly polished row of cars. Payback time for all the hours of hard work and measly pay checks. Maybe he was delirious from working in the sun all day? But he was last man standing on the car lot when he noticed the boss had left the office door open. He knew where the keys were kept, and he knew only too well which car his favourite was: the one he had cleaned and polished with the most care; the one he knew he would look real good in; the sapphire blue Pontiac Firebird.

And, sat behind the wheel, he did look good in it. And he had to go through with this. He turned the key and the engine roared into life. Double checking that the boss hadn't come back, he pulled off the forecourt and onto the eight-lane freeway out of downtown. Soon the suburbs were a distant vision in his rear-view mirror, and he was headed into the Nevada wilderness, destination Vegas.

He wound the windows down and put on the radio. Station KBRG playing classic hits full blast. He adjusted his shades, pulled down his cap and hit the gas pedal, barely believing what he'd done, as the tarmac strip disappeared behind him. He rarely left town, so the never-ending red desert stretching out on either side was like nothing he'd ever seen. The sun, low in the sky was casting long shadows from behind monolithic rocks and cactus trees. The black highway shimmered in the heat. His mind drifted to all the classic road movies he'd seen. He was Jack Kerouac, Bonnie and Clyde, Natural Born Killers all rolled into one.

Then he saw her.

Miles after mile of nothing. Not a single building, not another car. But there she was, plain as day, stood by the side of the road. Left hand holding a lit cigarette to her mouth. Right arm outstretched with an upturned thumb aimed straight at him. Even if he'd had any inclination to carry on driving, the Pontiac wasn't going to let him do anything but hit the brakes and pull over.

ODE TO DYLAN AND EDDIE

Do not do what they expect of you.
Break out of the bonds that trammel so tight.
Do what makes you happy, what's good for you.

Do only what you want to do.
Their prescriptive plots and plans aren't right.
They can't control you, can't tell you who

You ought to be, you have to be true
To your dreams, your fantasies, your fancies of flight.
Be the best you can be, the congruent you.

Dance like ecstasy has possessed you,
Laugh cacophonous laughter, burn long, burn bright,
Paint oceans orange and sunsets blue.

Sing 'til your lungs are empty, your cheeks are blue.
Run without touching the ground, shine the brightest light.
Love one, love many, love with all of you.

Leave your mark on this world, do it only for you.

Not for me, not for them, but for your own delight.

Be remembered forever, be the one who…

Do anything you want to do.

ON REGENT'S CANAL

The street bristled with activity, everyone in a hurry. Rushing to get home before the early nightfall the new season ushered in, the year hurtling day by day, week by week, towards the black hole of Christmas. A cyclist, a blur of fluorescent yellow, skidded her way precariously through piles of amber and umber leaves, ringing her bell frantically to clear an errant pedestrian from the road. The 274 bus splashed its way through ankle-deep water, puddled beneath the Camden Town railway bridge, drenching passers-by. The tube station spewed myriad shoppers and commuters onto the glistening pavement, coats and scarves brought out for the autumn, collars turned up against the chill evening air.

John Clark was one of the newly-deposited commuters. Only thirty-eight years old, but his face already pitted with lines of worry, his hair so thin, that he was obliged to wear a hat as early as October. Today had been particularly bad. Arriving at the office tired, irritable, and late, Laura from accounts had been giving him a hard time, and his boss was on at him about meaningless deadlines. A false alarm fire drill had taken half an hour out of his day, and he was falling further and further behind with his work. And at the end of the working day, he'd squeezed himself onto the tube, and spent the journey home rammed into the armpits of an accountant from Primrose Hill.

John hurried along Randolph Street, past Costa, and down the metal staircase, dropping gratefully into the haven that lies beneath the madness of street level. Here there was hardly a sound. The patter of joggers' footsteps, the whir of a bicycle and the occasional splash of a bird diving into the canal. Within three minutes he was clambering onto his nightly refuge, the narrow boat Rosie Lee.

SUNDOWN

In the Dreamtime, Yhi sleeps.

A whistle awakes

her, she walks the desert sand,

Beneath her feet it bakes.

Bathing the land in warmth

Soaking it in brilliant light.

Bringing new life to birth

Making day from night.

Her people stir too from slumber.

They worship the bountiful earth

But fear the blazing sun.

In harmony with both

Yhi's descendants displaced

By a new race of sun worshippers.

A noble people replaced

By surfers and skinny-dippers

Who pay no heed to Yhi.

She scorches their pale skin

As she scornfully watches them play

Where the mighty ocean rolls in.

Their cars pollute the air

Their rubbish chokes the sea.

The flames of rage burn hotter

On those who disrespect Yhi.

The fiery old sun sets.

The day lets out its final breath.

Yhi cries the earth to sleep

Another day closer to its death.

TASMANIA TRILOGY

PART ONE - WINEGLASS BAY

The peach-coloured sand stretched out as far as the eye could see. A narrow strip in the foreground, opening out into the broader, wineglass shape that gave the bay its name, the flats of the beach giving way to lush green, forested mountainside, crowned with a natural battlement of jagged rock formations.

Waves washed in from the Southern Ocean to one side, building up to form liquid mountains before crashing into a fizzing, frothing foam, dissipating into the hot sands, which sighed with cooling relief. On the other side, in the shelter of the bay, altogether more sedentary waters lapped and licked gently at the shoreline.

The sands were a table of red baize, ironed smooth by the actions of sea and wind. The extent of the high tide was evident from the ribbon of seaweed and shells that hemmed the beach. The relentless rhythm of the ocean turned this strip of sand from peach to cobalt and back again on a daily basis, cleansing it, restoring it, replenishing it, leaving behind new treasures scooped up from the deep.

Inland from the line of jetsam, the smooth sand quickly turned to rugged dunes. Piles of sand punctuated with knots of scrub and bush, burrows, and warrens. Rabbits and sandpipers darted in and out of the gaps in the vegetation, skilfully avoiding balls of tumbleweed being blown across the dunes by the Antarctic winds.

To the other side of the dunes was the calm of the bay. A serene seascape, its still waters returning a small fishing boat back to harbour, in its wake a flock of seabirds swooping and diving for afternoon scraps.

In the midst of all this stood a solitary human being. He eagerly drank it all in. He filled his lungs with the warm air, took in the smell of brine and let the taste of salt prickle and burst on his tongue. He listened in awe at the cacophony of nature: bursting waves; whistling wind and the chatter and chirruping of bird life. His eyes feasted on the palette of colours, and the striking contrast of light and shade, His imagination ran wild with seafaring adventures.

He felt glad to be alive.

PART TWO - A TASMANIAN CHRISTMAS

Christmas Day. Far from the comforting aroma of roast turkey and minced pies, he stood on the other side of the world, sun blazing down, looking out across a Tasmanian wilderness. It couldn't have been more different, but that was exactly what he had hoped for.

He breathed in again, rolling the air around in his nostrils and on his tongue like he was tasting a good wine, before taking the breath long and deep inside him. The air was unusually warm, and it dried his throat. At the back of his mouth he caught the sulphurous tang of dried seaweed, a hint of crab maybe, and the slightly burned smell of grass that had been baking under the sun for days. The smell was laced with sweetness, perhaps from the flower of one of the gorse-like bushes in the dunes, and he caught a very feint hint of diesel fumes from the distant trawler, which reminded him of his late father, a lorry driver for forty years. Then the breeze changed direction and brought down from the mountain with it an overpowering wave of eucalyptus, all cough sweets and chest rub. The combination of scents and aromas was as complex as the bouquet of any wine.

The change of wind direction changed the soundscape, which was remarkably vibrant for a supposed wilderness. Instead of the scouring and crashing of wave upon wave, slapping and smoothing the sandy shore, he could now hear the chug-chug-chug of the trawler's engine, its constant rhythm interrupted by the clanking of winches bringing the nets in from the water, slightly out of time with the engine noises, like the percussion section of an avant-garde jazz band. Accompanying the band, seagulls squawked and wailed a hungry, haunting tune to accompany their feeding frenzy.

PART THREE - THE RESCUE

The northerly wind brought with it the sounds and smells of dry land rather than the maritime noises and aromas carried on the sea breeze. It was the smell he noticed first. The soothing, medicinal scent of eucalyptus gave way to a hint of scout camp and the trouble he and Mike had got into burning all the firewood on the first night. He assumed his mind was playing psychosomatic tricks on him, but as he recovered his focus, he realised the acrid smoke smell that had invaded his nose was real.

His ears pricked up, his heightened senses working in unison. Instead of the soft music of the sea, he heard violent whip-cracks ripping down the mountainside. Above the trawler jazz, the shrieking of seagulls gradually morphed into a human voice crying frantically for help.

Quickly and instinctively, he used the sounds and smells to triangulate the source of the cries. They were coming from the dunes, between him and the bayside shoreline. They were growing louder and more desperate. He threw off his backpack and took out his water bottles and two large towels. He ran to the sea and immersed himself and the towels in the water, which was still quite cold despite it being December in the Southern Hemisphere. He cloaked himself in the wet towels, and, without a thought for his own safety, ran through the wall of fire that now engulfed the dunes. The heat and smell were unbearable. He almost retched as he took in a lungful of thick, hot smoke. The roar of the flames devouring the tinderbox gorse bushes was deafening. He was beginning to lose all hope when, in a clearing in the dunes, he found the young mother and her daughter, lying flat on the ground under a picnic blanket, their cries drowned out by the crackling of the flames.

'Here, put these around you,' he said as he threw his towels towards them. 'We can't go back towards the ocean; the only way out is through there.' He pointed towards the bay, which could just be seen intermittently through the clouds of smoke and flames. 'Keep close to the ground and be as quick as you can.'

The three of them held on to each other as they snaked blindly through the dunes and towards safety. The air became cleaner; the smell of burning bush subsided. The discordant thundering of the rampant fire subdued and, as they clambered into the refuge of the bayside beach, they once again heard the familiar jazz syncopation of the trawler pulling up to rescue them.

THE CALVARY AT ST YVES

A long, hot summer stutters to a close

Unsure if it wants to turn to Autumn

Or blaze on for a week or two longer.

A picnic unfolded at the side of the road

A car crash of linen and wicker.

Cheese too runny, wine too warm,

Bread stale before its time.

We wait for the pardon parade to come.

A drummer shatters the silence with a staccato rhythm.

A solitary piper holds a drone chord

And an accordion player squeezes life into a timeless tune.

First the menfolk march into view.

Centuries of tradition carved into their sun blasted faces.

Then the women.

Lace creations on their heads, bobbing

Like waves of whitecaps breaking on a Breton beach.

Dignified faces remind us this is a saint's day.

The parade has passed almost as soon as it arrived.

This is a small but proud village

Its numbers dwindling year on year,

Its youth stolen by the bright lights of Rennes, of Nantes, of Paris.

Its elderly returned to the soil in equal numbers.

Picnic gathered up and loaded onto bicycles

We pedal in pursuit of the parade.

Along the dusty track to the Calvary

A towering, geometric edifice to St Yves.

A priest recites holy words

Not in the tongue of my O Level French books

But in a Breton dialect more akin to Cornish or Welsh.

The locals listen in reverence, bowing their heads in prayer.

The tourists watch on in tolerance, eagerly awaiting the trumpet call

Which finally comes to signal the start of the feast.

Crepes burst with the fragrance of cheese and ham and exotic mushrooms,

Sausages sizzle in a pan big enough to bathe in,

Bread, oh, the smell of freshly baked bread

And apple cider and calvados flowing freely.

The band sheds its funereal skin and strikes up a lively jig.

Waistcoated men take their women

And fling them in impeccable time

Until their towering headgear nearly come off.

Visitors eat, drink, and clap their hands

But keep a respectful distance from the dance floor.

Nobody has noticed dusk creeping in

But the glowing sun slowly dips below the distant orchards

And evening falls on this unremarkable corner of Brittany.

And the music plays on.

THE FIRST DAY OF SPRING

The unmistakeable sounds of spring. The thwack of bat on ball. A ripple of applause circumnavigating the ground. A solitary, raucous cry of 'shot' from the members' bar. The stuttering clank of a vintage mechanical scoreboard. The murmur of appreciative conversation in the pavilion, fading to respectful silence. A communal sharp intake of breath. Thundering footsteps as the lean paceman gallops in. A yelp as he releases the ball, the faintest tickle of willow on leather, then the dull thud as the 'keeper gloves it. 'Owzat?' the collective cry, then another ripple of applause as the umpire raises a single finger to consign the batsman back to the pavilion.

Visually striking too. In these first days of the season, the backdrop is more often leaden skies than blazing sunshine. Bulbous thunderclouds providing a stark contrast to the starched white of county sweaters, flannel pants with razor sharp creases, flapping in stiff spring breezes coming in off the seas from Hove to Scarborough. White sight screens tower above lush green outfields, allowing batsmen, with their eyesight not yet attuned to the new season, to pick out the red dot hurtling towards them at breakneck speed. Early season crowds sparse but enthusiastic. A confused smattering of shorts and t-shirts, symbols of spring optimism, mixed with chunky jumpers and brightly coloured cagoules. Tartan picnic blankets, wicker hampers, glasses of straw-coloured lager vie with silver thermos flasks of warming coffee.

All the smells of spring return too. The scent of willow soaked in linseed oil competes with deep heat and other exotic balms, applied to cold muscles to ward off the bitter weather. The outfield, freshly cut, releases its seductive aroma. The chill air carries the waft of a hot dog stand from behind the grandstand. Two small children covered in coconut scented sun block - more in hope than expectation. Salt in the air reminds us the seaside is not far away, too early in the season to be busy yet. The groundsman starts up his quad bike, releasing a cloud of diesel fumes, as he drags the heavy roller across the outfield.

More than all of this, a unique language comes out of hibernation. Googlies are delivered. The corridor of uncertainty is explored. Square leg is fine, fine leg is deep and third man is stood with his legs apart waiting for a tickle. The poetry of John Arlott, the vocal artistry of Richie Benaud, Geoffrey Boycott telling it exactly how it is. A number seventy-three bus goes past the Vauxhall End and the listeners have sent in more cake.

It's spring. Move over football, cricket is back. An England of a different age has returned, if only for a few precious months.

THE MEN'S ROOM

Let me in, she said.

No, I won't, he replied.

But I really want

To know what's inside.

I don't know who you are.

I can't let you in.

Who I am, who I am?

Where do I begin?

I'm my mother's daughter,

And my daughter's mother.

I'm my twin's twin.

I'm me, she's the other.

That's no use to me.

Give me a name.

Give me a number.

This isn't a game.

I'm the raiser of children.

I'm the keeper of man.

I'm a cook, I'm a cleaner.

That's who I am.

That's not good enough.

You still can't come in.

Give me a reason.

My patience is thin.

I'm the shoulder they cry on.

The balm for their aches.

The mender of trousers.

The baker of cakes.

The midnight taxi,

The morning alarm.

I see that they're fed

And come to no harm.

The teller of stories.

The pusher of prams.

The kisser of foreheads.

The holder of hands.

That's quite a list, madame.

And all well and good.

But 'Men only' it says.

No women allowed.

You could be a troublemaker.

You'll just have to go.

No, I'm not, she said,

As far as I know.

I will let you in,

You've made a good case.

Go take a look, and

Please check out the place.

You know what, I won't.

I'd rather not be

In a room with no women,

That's just not for me.

I'll stay here, outside.

I'd rather not bother.

I'll be who I am,

A daughter, a mother…

TOO OLD TO ROCK AND ROLL

PART ONE – ROCK AND ROLL NIGHTS, ROCK AND ROLL DAYS

Ed sharpened into semi-consciousness and surveyed the wreckage of the hotel room, trying to piece together the events of the previous night. An empty Jack Daniels bottle stood on the bedside table. 'When in Rome,' he thought, but its emptiness was clearly not a good sign. Nor was the sight of two – not one, but two – empty glasses next to it. Next to the bedside table stood the new cowboy boots that he'd bought in the Cowboy Corner store downtown yesterday. He loved them at first sight and they simply had to be worn on stage. He hoped he'd done them justice. The weather had been warm for the time of year – twenty-five degrees (or seventy-seven as the Yanks liked to say) – and dry – he recalled hearing on the radio that people had been killed in a dust storm in San Francisco.

    He started to recall the gig at the newly opened 3rd & Lindsley concert hall. They'd sold out all one thousand tickets. Not bad for a bunch of Welsh boys. He remembered it being a good show – they'd been on form. As well as playing blues and country to satisfy the locals' taste, they'd cheekily squeezed in a Freddie Mercury tribute number. He vaguely remembered screaming. And girls. Lots of girls. He looked across the room again and saw his hastily discarded black shirt, black jeans, black cowboy hat. Then something that didn't belong. Knickers. Pink knickers.

    'Oh my God, Connie,' he thought to himself. 'What time is it back in Merthyr?'

    He thought of his wife back home with Alfie, who was now three years old. She was six months pregnant with what they knew would be Alfie's sister. It was cold back home. He was missing the Rugby World Cup, but he didn't care. Wales were out, and as long as England lost the final, he was happy. Ed couldn't find his watch, so he switched on the radio.

'You're listening to WHRK radio and here is the news at eleven o'clock. President George W. H. Bush welcomes the latest troops back from the Gulf...'

He quickly turned it off again.

'Good. Eleven a.m. here, that means five in the afternoon over there,' he thought. He picked up the bedside phone and dialled through to reception.

'I'd like to make a call to the UK please.'

Later that day, Ed sat at the poolside bar in the Crowne Plaza, his feet dipped tentatively in the water in that very British way. Sticking to local tradition, his drink of choice was a Whiskey Sour, and it was going some way towards soothing the previous night's hangover.

'Better take it easy though,' he thought, 'soundcheck in an hour, and then another sell-out show.'

He was minded to pinch himself as he reflected on their crazy journey from playing the working men's clubs in the South Wales valleys, sleeping in the back of the van, and now here they were in downtown Memphis, home and resting place of the King of Rock 'n' Roll himself.

The hangover wasn't the only thing he was hoping to take the edge off with his Whiskey Sour. He hadn't entirely pieced together the previous night, and large parts of it remained a mystery to him. The conversation with Connie earlier had been difficult. The crackly transatlantic line hadn't helped, and he was convinced she could hear his guilt in every sentence. It had been good to hear her voice – but in a way that had focused his guilt even more sharply. The hardest part was when she'd put Alfie on the line. He really missed that boy, missed watching him grow up, and he wondered how long he could juggle the touring lifestyle with being a family man. It wouldn't be long now until his family increased in size, and he knew in his heart that this would probably be his one and only visit to Memphis.

Ed's thoughts were interrupted by the sound of splashing water. After a short delay, a bow wave lapped at his feet to remind him that poolside bars weren't just for drinking in. The pool's new arrival completed a width underwater and surfaced at Ed's feet.

'Hey Mister Bassman,' the girl said in a seductive Tennessee drawl, as she swept her dark wet hair from her face. 'Will you play for me again tonight?'

Ed had a sudden vision of very skimpy pink knickers and choked on his Whiskey Sour.

PART TWO - AUF WIEDERSEHEN, CONNIE

The suitcase sat on the bed next to the Fender bass in its battered black case. It looked way too big for the few things that were in it. They both stared at it in awkward silence.

'You're actually going through with it then.' His wife was the first to speak.

'You know I have to. It's only for a few weeks.'

'At your age, really. Driving round Germany in the middle of winter. Sleeping in the back of that battered old van. I just don't get it.'

'No, you never did. Look, when Pete and Jim said they were getting the band back together, I just couldn't say no.'

'And never mind what I think, I'm only your wife after all.'

The bedroom door slammed the conversation shut. The suitcase zip opened up a whole world of doubt.

'Am I too old for these black shirts? Too fat for these black jeans?' he thought to himself. He took them out and put them on the bed, but immediately refolded them and placed them back in the case.

'I might not be old snake hips anymore, but I reckon I can still get away with them.'

He continued to shuffle around the contents of the worn old case.

'That hat looked good back in the day. Ha, the boots. I remember buying them in Nashville and wearing them on stage the same night. What a gig that was.'

His mind drifted back thirty years to when his waistline was smaller, his hair longer and his fingers a lot nimbler.

'Sunglasses on stage? Indoors? Ah why not? But she's right. We're crashing in the back of the van this time. No budget for hotels. How am I going to sleep with Pete and Jim banging on all night? Once Pete starts one of his stories there's no stopping him.'

He remembered the travel pack he got on the last long-haul flight he'd taken. Not with the band, but with the family, when they went out to Australia to visit their son and grandchildren. They were happy days too, but they just didn't give him the buzz that went with being on stage. The anticipation of that first note. The relief as the opening chords burst out of the speakers. The roar of adulation from the crowd. Nonetheless, into the case went the inflatable neck pillow, the earplugs and the Qantas sleeping mask.

'And I'm not going to sleep in my boots and hat, am I?'

He chucked a couple of pairs of comfy joggers and a few t-shirts haphazardly into the case.

'Maybe I am getting too old for this?'

He looked at his gnarled fingers, twisted and calloused from years of fret work. He took the bottle of Jack Daniels out of the case and placed it on the bedside table. In its place went a hefty novel and a pack of playing cards.

'Rock and roll,' he laughed.

PART THREE – A LETTER FROM BERLIN

Berlin, 4th February.

My Dearest Connie

You know how much I hate to admit I was wrong. Even more so when it means acknowledging you were right. But I was wrong, and you were right.

It's been awful out here. Dan, our so-called manager, promised the Germans would be mad for us, but who wants to listen to a bunch of old men playing the blues, badly? Pete's voice is shot, and Jim can barely hold down a chord. I'm not quite as bad as them. As you know, I've still been playing on and off over the years, but I can't carry the others. What were we thinking? You can't turn back the clock just by putting on some black clothes and a pair of sunglasses – it doesn't work like that.

You can't blame me for giving it a go though. I mean there has to be more to life than working in that factory. We had some great times, back in the day, some good laughs, and I guess we just wanted one more shot at that. Remember that time we got kicked out of rehearsing in the church hall after Pete nearly burned the place down? We had to change our name from the Holy to the Unholy Trinity! And they *were* great times. Remember when we toured the States, and you came out to see us?

I know you think I've resented you all these years for making me give it all up to start the family. But honestly, that's not true. I always said when I met you, that when the time came, I'd settle down in The Valley with you and the kids. I don't regret that for one moment. The day our Alfie came into the world was the best day of my life, well second to the day I met you. I just wish they lived nearer, and we could see them more often – or that Dan could swing us a reunion tour to Australia.

Darling, there is something I have to tell you. It can't wait until I get back, and I just couldn't tell you on the phone.

Pete and I had a massive falling out when we were in Hamburg. We were tired from a long day on the road, and we'd both had a few beers too many. It got personal and I said something about his wife that I shouldn't have. You know that me and Penny had a bit of a fling before I met you, and way before she met Pete. Well, what I haven't told you is it happened again after our Ben was born. I know it's no excuse, but you were tired and preoccupied with the new baby. I didn't know what to do with myself around the house – whatever I tried to do was wrong and you just snapped at me all the time. I felt excluded – it was you and the kids, and I was on the outside. Anyway, Pete was away working, and Penny gave me a shoulder to cry on… and, well, you can guess the rest.

I know this doesn't make it any easier, but it was a long time ago and nothing has happened since, not with Penny or anyone else. Nor will it ever happen again. You are the only one for me and always will be. Pete and I had it out, and we're back on speaking terms again, but it's all still a bit awkward. I am so, so sorry and I desperately hope you can forgive me. I'm sure we can work this out.

And so here I am sitting in a dreary grey café in Berlin, drinking lukewarm coffee and watching the snow fall. Tonight, I've got to sleep in a van with two snoring and farting old men. I've made some terrible mistakes and I beg you to forgive me for them.

I miss you terribly and I have never felt so cold.

Ed.

PART FOUR – CONNIE REPLIES

Merthyr, 11th February.

Dear Ed

I got your letter from Berlin. I hope your manager is able to forward this on to you, wherever in Europe you are now.

It sounds truly awful for you and the guys over there, and for a while I had some sympathy for you.

But let's be honest here. The real reason you are touring Germany in a clapped-out old van and playing to a handful of people in decrepit Bierkellers is simply this. You have never grown up, and you probably never will. You mentioned the incident in the church hall. Why bring that up now? You were eighteen. God dammit you still think you're eighteen now. You've never left behind that young lad kicking a tin can round the streets of Merthyr. I'll admit, that's part of why I fell for you in the first place, your boyish charms, but you're fifty-nine now. You have responsibilities. You have children, grandchildren. You have me! You should be at home in your slippers, watching TV with your wife and a cup of tea, not dressed from head to toe in black, playing the blues, swilling German bier and no doubt chasing the first Fraulein who makes a play for you.

You sound full of remorse in your letter, but I'm not sure I'm buying it. Why did you have to bring up the thing with Pete's wife? Yes, I'm glad that you and he have got it all out in the open and that you're trying to repair the damage that was done. But did you think for one moment, the effect it would have on me to see all that written down in a letter? Of course, you didn't! You don't have the emotional maturity to think of anyone but yourself.

So please don't write to me again. I need time to think things through, and I think you do too. I don't know how I feel at the moment, or even how I will feel when you get home, but we'll talk then. And I need it to be a grown-up conversation, with a fifty-nine-year-old man. With my husband.

You have never felt so cold.

I have never felt so alone.

Yours, Connie

PART FIVE - BOYS IN THE BAND

Ed had enjoyed his time in Germany, and he had met some great people, but now he was looking forward to going home and to sleeping in his own bed. He had arrived at Bremerhaven and prepared to check in. Unfortunately, there was no record of his booking, so he approached the desk to raise the problem with the representative.

'Entschuldigen Sie mir bitte,' he said in a strange Merthyr dialect of German. 'Sprechen Sie Englisch?'

'Ja, naturlich. Yes, of course.' The ferry company representative was a younger woman, probably in her mid-twenties. Her heavy make-up and well sculpted blonde hair complemented perfectly her navy-blue corporate outfit. She looked more than a match for a tired and disoriented, elderly Welshman.

'Good, because there's been a mix up, and I'm buggered if I'm explaining it in German.' His accent had returned to pure Valleys now.

Her smile persisted, a barrier against the impending onslaught.

'So, we, that's me and my mates Pete and Jim, you can call us The Unholy Trinity, if you like.'

'Unholy, was ist das?' The Teutonic defences were starting to crack.

'Oh, The Unholy Trinity,' Ed continued, 'we're a band. You know, blues, rock and roll. We were pretty famous back in the day. Toured all over Europe, America too. But you don't need to know that. What you do need to know is that Pete and

Jim are booked on the next ferry, the eleven-hundred to Felixstowe, and so is our van with all our kit in it. But I'm not.'

'You will speak more slowly please. You are famous Musikante, how you say, musician?'

'Well, yes, kind of, I'm the bass player, but that's not the issue here. The issue is that I'm not booked on the next ferry, and I want to get back to Wales, to my wife, to my bed. Well, probably not to me wife, she's going to bloody kill me, but definitely to my bed. We've been on the road for nine weeks and I'm shattered. Hamburg, Dortmund, Düsseldorf...'

'Ach, zu schnell, you must please just say me the facts,' the representative said. 'You want to make ferry to Wales, yes? Where is this Wales? We only make ferry to England. Can you explain please, Mister...?'

'Legg. Ed Legg. Aka Snake Hips Stevens,' he said, unhelpfully.

'Please? Your name is Legg-ed-legg? Your name is Stevens? What *is* Snake Hips?'

Ed peered at her name badge whilst trying to avoid staring at the cleavage she seemed keen to display. FRAULEIN USCHI BIERHOFF.

'OK listen, Fraulein Uschi Bierhoff. My name is Edward Legg. E-D-W-A-R-D L-E-G-G. I am supposed to be on the eleven-hundred ferry from Bremerhaven to Felixstowe but the ticket we have just says two passengers – Jim Wood and Pete Llewelyn – and a Ford Transit. There must be some mistake, can you check please?'

'Ah, ja, sehr gut, I am understanding you now,' said Fraulein Uschi Bierhoff, 'Herr. Legg. Let me just check the Reservieren system.'

The frantic tapping of keys was followed by a not very reassuring look on the German's face.

'I'm sorry, Herr Legg. There is no booking for you. Only booking for Herr Wood and Herr – how you say – Loo-wa-lin. And the Ford Transit, this a van, ja?'

'Ja, yes. But there must be some mistake,' Ed pleaded. 'How am I going to get home?'

'I can reserve you on the next available ferry. You will like this?' she asked.

'Yes please,' said Ed.

More keyboard tapping followed, then Fraulein Uschi Bierhoff looked up.

'The next ferry you can travel ist... hier, Freitag, on Friday at oh-four-hundred,' she said.

'But today's Wednesday, and that's an ungodly hour.'

'And you will pay two-hundred-and-fifty Euros,' she continued.

'How much?' Ed was beginning to panic now. 'But I've only got a hundred Euros, and I'll need to find somewhere to stay for two nights. Some rock and roll reunion this has turned out to be.'

Ed turned his back on the service desk and headed back towards his band mates.

'Hang on a minute, did you two know about this?'

PART SIX – SNAKE HIPS RETURNS

As the train pulled into Merthyr, Ed could see Connie waiting on the platform. A thousand thoughts ran through his head as he picked up his bass and hold-all and stepped off the train.

'Hiya love,' he said more in hope than expectation.

'Don't you bloody 'hiya love' me. Where the hell have you been? The others got back on Wednesday. Couple of extra days with your fancy woman was it?'

'Wait… what fancy woman. I couldn't get on the ferry. Didn't the others tell you?'

'No, they didn't,' she said. 'Not that I'd waste my time talking to those two clowns.'

'Look, there isn't any fancy woman. I told you everything in my letter.'

'Don't mention that bloody letter,' Connie said. 'You've got a nerve showing up here after that. Didn't you get my letter?'

'No. What letter love?'

'Less of the 'love.' I told you what I thought in my letter.'

'Well I'm sorry, I never got a letter. You're here to meet me though, aren't you? That must mean something?'

'Wanted to give you a piece of my mind. Don't you think you're getting away with this.'

'But love…'

'What did I just tell you?'

'Sorry. But Connie. Can't we just talk? Please?'

Connie replied with a nod of her head, in the direction of the empty waiting room.

'In there. You've got five minutes. You'd better make it good.'

Ed opened the door and motioned Connie towards the wooden bench. It looked as hard and uncompromising as she did. He leaned his bass against the wall, sat down next to Connie – not too close – and put down his hold-all in the no-man's-land between them.

'Well first I want to say how truly sorry I am for causing you so much upset. I'm sorry for what I did at the time, and I'm sorry that I've dragged it all out into the open again.'

'So you bloody should be. It's a start, go on...'

'It was a long time ago, nearly twenty years. It was a one-off, I swear. Nothing like it has happened since, you have to believe me. There were girls throwing themselves at us in Germany...'

Connie's face cracked a smile for the first time.

'Don't laugh, there were,' Ed continued, 'but I didn't so much as look at any of them. None of us did.'

'Keep going.' The deadpan had returned.

'You're the only one for me. Always have been – apart from one moment of madness...'

'Two moments of madness,' she interrupted.

'...apart from two moments of madness – and you always will be. You and the kids. The house. Merthyr. That means everything to me. Everything. I've been a bloody idiot,

I know. I've probably lost my best friend over this; I don't want to lose you too. I must have been mad thinking I could be "old Snake Hips" again. All I want is to come home to you and, you know, be old, act my age. Please give me that chance.'

The moment's silence lasted thirty-five years. It lasted nine weeks. It stretched from Merthyr to Memphis and all over Germany.

'You daft bugger,' she said and kicked the hold-all out of the way, cwtching up to him. 'Black always did suit you.'

PART SEVEN - BE MY VALENTINE

Jim ordered two pints of bitter and took them over to a table in a quiet corner of the Golden Lion, where Ed was sat waiting. In fact, it was a Tuesday afternoon in Merthyr, so all of the corners of the pub were fairly quiet. The third chair at the table remained empty.

'Cheers,' said Jim.

'Cheers,' said Ed, 'thanks for agreeing to see me.'

Ed took a long drink from his pint glass, quickly followed by another. He cleared his throat, loudly, both to settle his nerves and to emphasise the importance of what he was about to say.

'So, what did happen at Bremerhaven? Did you two have anything to do with that ticket fiasco?' Ed asked.

'Look I'm sorry mate. It was Pete really. He said it was bad enough spending all that time together in Germany. He just couldn't stomach the three of us together on the ferry crossing.'

'You mean he couldn't stand the thought of being with me on the boat?'

'Yeah, something like that,' Jim said, sipping his beer much more slowly than Ed had his. 'Look, it was wrong, and I'm really sorry. If you're out of pocket, you know, with your fare and accommodation and that, let me know. There's a bit of money in the kitty. Not much, but it should cover most of it.'

'Thanks mate,' said Ed, that's really generous. I think I'm going to need it, too.'

Ed had finished his pint already. German beer was fine, but you couldn't beat a pint of Brains.

'Another?' He asked.

'Oh, go on then,' Jim replied.

'So, where do we stand then?' asked Ed, returning with two more drinks.

'Well, I still want us to keep going,' Jim said, 'I didn't think the tour went that badly. But I don't know if Pete wants to be in the same room as you, let alone play in a band with you.'

'Oh, like that is it? You know what, that suits me fine. See I was thinking it was time to call it quits.'

'Really? I thought...'

Ed interrupted. 'Look, none of us are getting any younger, and we were pretty ropey for some of those gigs. And then there's Connie.'

'Ah yes, I meant to ask you how things were on the home front.'

'Well, I think she's forgiven me, for now, but there's got to be some big changes. Like the band, for example. I don't think she'll accept me going back on the road any time soon, if ever.'

'Fair enough.'

'Which brings me on to money. How much do you reckon I've got tied up in the band? I mean if we sold up all our gear.'

'A couple of grand, maybe more. But you can't be serious.'

'And the van?' Ed asked.

'Oh, you are serious. Well that's worth about five grand I suppose.'

'So, enough for what I've got in mind then. Drink up mate.'

Both men finished their beers and headed off in different directions at the door of the Lion.

Ed's first stop was the florists. Lilies were Connie's favourites, and together with Gemma, who as well as being an incredibly talented florist, was also one of the Unholy Trinity's biggest fans, he put together an arrangement that was guaranteed to melt Connie's heart.

'And you can definitely deliver them for Thursday? Ed asked.

'Yes sure,' said Gemma, 'and I'll do you mate's rates. Good luck.'

Emboldened by this success, he sat on the bench outside the florist and got out his phone. They would be just waking up in Australia, so he fired off a quick text to Alfie.

'Just checking. Still OK for the dates I mentioned yesterday? Dad.'

The response came back in seconds. Sometimes Ed was amazed by technology.

'Yes sure. Good luck.'

Next port of call that afternoon was the Italian restaurant. It had always been Connie's favourite and they'd had many memorable evenings there. Luigi knew them both really well, and he'd be sure to make certain everything went smoothly.

'Afternoon, Luigi,' Ed called, cheerfully.

'Bongiorno,' Luigi replied.

'Just making sure everything's good for Thursday.'

'Of course. Just leave it to me.'

Ed's final stop that afternoon was the travel agents at the end of the high street. This was going to be the riskiest part of the plan. It was a lot of money, money he didn't have right now, and he had no way of knowing whether he could sell his gear in time to be able to fly out before the end of the Australian summer. But he had enough for the deposit, so he'd be able to at least present an itinerary to Connie on Thursday, even if he couldn't actually hand over the tickets. He knew he had to take this chance, or risk losing the woman he loved. He took a deep breath, and a furtive look around to make sure no one was watching, and he pulled open the travel agent's door...

That was it. All booked. Ed couldn't recall a time when he'd felt so nervous. Not on his wedding day. Not on stage in front of thousands of fans. Not ever. His instinct was to return to the Golden Lion to calm the butterflies, but he knew that wasn't a good idea. The last thing he wanted to do was to turn up half cut and start a row with Connie, now that things were back on a relatively good footing again. The house on Tudor Street was in darkness when he arrived home.

'That's funny,' he thought, 'Connie is usually home by now.' He opened the front door, and he was overwhelmed by the smell of something good coming from the slow cooker. But no Connie. He turned on the downstairs lights one by one. The small kitchen, beginning to look a little tired now, was empty.

'Hmmm. Could have got a new kitchen for the cost of those flights.'

He tried the living room. He'd decorated last year, so it looked presentable, but the three-piece suite gave off a guilty look of well-worn brown leather shoes, rather than the straight-out-of-the-showroom shine it once had.

'Connie, love, are you home?' he called.

No reply, so he kicked off his shoes, hung up his jacket in the hallway and headed upstairs. The main bedroom looked inviting once more, how a married couple's bedroom should look, all fluffed up pillows and flowery warmth. He stuck his head round the door of what had been Alfie's room before he emigrated. A recently-used sleeping bag on the bed reminded Ed of the less warm welcome he'd got on his return from Germany.

The sound of the front door opening downstairs interrupted his thoughts.

'Ed, is that you love?' Connie called up the stairs.

'Yes, where have you been? he replied.

'Oh, err; I just had to pop out. Dinner's in the slow cooker, it won't be long.'

Ed heard shuffling and rustling, and the banging of cupboard doors. He rushed down the stairs. Connie looked flustered, and it was a rosy cheek that Ed kissed affectionately.

'I didn't expect you to be here,' she said.

'Pleasantly surprised I hope?'

'Of course,' she said. 'Love, have you, err, got anything planned for Thursday night? You know what day it is?'

'I have, as it happens, but it's a surprise.'

'Oh good,' Connie said, looking over Ed's shoulder to make sure she'd shut the cupboard properly. 'But I hope you haven't gone mad.'

'You'll have to wait and see,' he said.

The lamb stew that came out of the slow cooker tasted every bit as good as it smelled.

'That was delicious love,' he said, 'You know I'd be happy to stay in on Thursday if you can rustle up something else as good as that.'

'I thought you had something planned?'

'I have,' he laughed, 'I'm only teasing.'

'You can do the dishes for that!'

Just as Ed turned the taps full on, and started clattering dishes around, Connie's mobile rang.

'Can't you do that quietly?'

She took the call in the living room, but Ed overheard the occasional snippet. 'Yes,' 'Good,' 'When can you do it?' and, 'Will it fit in there?' interrupted the sound of bubbly water washing over white dinner plates.

Thursday came and they dressed for the occasion. Ed in his best suit – black, of course – and a black shirt with metal tipped collars and a bootlace tie. Connie looked fifteen years younger, Ed thought, in the floral dress she'd chosen. They held hands as they made the short walk to Luigi's.

'Ah good evening. Connie you look beautiful, and Ed, what can I say?' Luigi greeted them with his usual warmth, which although not sounding genuine, was actually heartfelt. They had been friends for many years. He showed them to their table. Ed gallantly pulled out a chair for Connie and waited until she was seated before he sorted himself out. They both ordered a seafood starter which arrived at the table presently. Just as Connie lifted her first forkful, Gemma arrived at the table with a huge bouquet of lilies.

'Connie, these are for you. Have a lovely evening the pair of you,' Gemma said.

'Oh, they're beautiful Ed,' Connie said, a huge grin across her youthful looking face.

Ed blushed. 'Only the best for you love'

Ed had ordered steak and Connie the medallions of lamb. They sat drinking a smooth grenache as they waited for the main course to arrive.

'This is lovely, Ed, thank you,' she said.

'Just like old times,' said Ed.

'Ed,' Connie continued, 'I've got a little surprise for you. Well actually it's not that little.'

'Wait, I've got one for you too,' he said.

'Oh really, you shouldn't have. You go first then.'

Ed reached into his inside jacket pocket and pulled out an envelope. He passed it across the table to Connie, who opened it excitedly. Inside was the booking confirmation from the travel agents: flights to Sydney in April. Connie wiped a tear from her eye as she read the words on the page.

'Oh, Ed, it's perfect,' she said, 'but how can we afford it?'

'Don't you worry about that,' he reassured her, perhaps not very convincingly. 'Anyway, never mind that, what have you got me?'

Connie clicked her fingers to summon Luigi across.

'Now please, Luigi.'

The restaurant owner opened the large cupboard behind the bar, to reveal a brand-new Fender bass and amplifier, the exact make and model Ed had always wanted.

'Darling, I've got something to tell you,' he said.

TYPEWRITER, POSSESSED

Rat-tat-tat. Rat-tat-tat-tat-tat. Thud. Rat-tat-tat-tat-tat ding, whirr. Crumple, rustle, rustle (pause) pad-doom.

'Yes, get in. I might not be able to write, but I'd still give the Harlem Globetrotters a run for their money at wastepaper bin basketball.'

Jeff loaded another sheet of pristine A4 into the typewriter and stared at it, trying to impress his thoughts onto the vast whiteness by power of telekinesis.

'Why am I doing this?' he said to himself, 'I must be mad.' He glanced at his watch. 2.35. AM. 'More coffee.'

Jeff tiptoed to the kitchen. Writer's block was bad, but not as bad as the grief he'd get if he woke Helen.

He took a mug down from the cupboard, the kind that had a door that, the harder you tried to open it quietly, the noisier it was determined to be. He heaped in one, no two, teaspoons of Nescafe and willed the kettle to boil quietly. It didn't. Neither did he yelp quietly when he poured boiling water on his hand.

'Shit. Bugger. Bollocks,' he said over the clanking of teaspoon against porcelain. He dare not open the fridge door. 'Black coffee it is then.'

'Why am I doing this?' he thought again as he sat back down in the study. 'It's stupid o'clock. Normal people are in bed now, yet here I am.' He pushed the typewriter to one side.

'Too noisy,' he thought, 'and that blank sheet of paper is far too intimidating.' He pulled the laptop out of the draw and fired it up. He opened up Word and found it was just as easy to stare at a blank screen as it was a virgin sheet of paper.

It was true he had had his publisher on the phone earlier in the day, reminding him that he'd already had an advance, and that it was about time he had something to show for it.

But that wasn't what was making him burn the candle at both ends. He knew he was sitting on a goldmine with these stories. The public couldn't get enough of them, and there was plenty more money forthcoming from the publishers if he could just bang out another episode or two. But that wasn't it. He was comfortably off, had everything he really needed. He wasn't driven by money.

It was also true that he was very much in the doghouse with Helen, without waking her up with his kitchen goings on, and it was altogether much easier if they didn't share the same bed at the moment.

He knew the adrenaline buzz he got from writing. The thrill of putting pen to paper, bringing characters to life, of committing the stories to paper. He knew all that, but that wasn't why, either. At the end of the day, he knew he was just compelled to write. He had a story that had to be told and tell it he would.

Jeff finished his coffee, turned back to the laptop, and began to type. And once he began, he couldn't stop.

VEGANUARY

Tony woke up on New Year's Day with a head like blancmange and a mouth like someone had been cleaning his tongue with the toilet brush. 'Fifty-five years on this planet and I still haven't learned,' he said to himself, as he surveyed the landscape of empty bottles and glasses. '2019 is going to be different!' He wracked his brain thinking of what he could do for this year's Resolution. Give up drink was the obvious one. No. Way too drastic. Run a marathon. No. Been there, done that, and besides, his limbs and muscles were not getting any younger. Just then a trailer came on the TV for a programme called Dirty Vegan. Now there's an idea. Killing fewer animals seemed quite appealing, as did a more sustainable food chain. There were obvious health benefits. But the clinching argument was, even after 32 years as a vegetarian, he didn't quite feel smug enough, and this was a great way to push that boundary a bit further.

His first thought was to do some research. He googled 'Veganuary' and it all seemed quite achievable. He messaged Sally. She'd been Vegan for years. She looked healthy enough. She ran marathons and hadn't packed up and left for a monastery just yet. He checked out the fridge. Okay, so there was some milk, and cheese, and a few eggs. 'How about I don't start until I've cleared the house of bad things,' he thought. That seemed like a reasonable compromise, after all, everyone started their resolutions on 1st January, and Tony always liked to be a bit different. And besides, Dirty Vegan wasn't on TV for a couple of days yet.

Monday turned to Tuesday, and the eggs were gone. Tuesday turned to Wednesday, and all the Christmas cheeses were eaten. The honey (yes, exploitation of innocent bees is a thing) ran out on Thursday, and by the weekend there was only one thing left – the Christmas Baileys! Tony allowed himself one last fling as he consumed the milky treat on Friday night, and by Saturday, he was a vegan!

Now, a week later, and Tony was still on the vegan path. There had been trials and tribulations along the way. How on earth do you pronounce "quinoa" let alone cook it? How long would it take to acquire a taste for rubbery vegan cheese? And where was he going to find a vegan beer? Toughest of all – breaking the news to the kids. However, after a week of being a not so Dirty Vegan, Tony definitely feels a little healthier, his kids hate him, but he definitely feels a lot more smug than he did at the beginning of the year!

WHY I WRITE (ARTURO'S OPUS)

It took every ounce of energy that he had. He strained his neck muscles and willed his head closer and closer to the monitor until finally the pointer attached to his head made a soft contact with the screen, and the device responded with a slightly robotic middle C. He collapsed back onto the bed, red as a sunset, sweating profusely, and contemplated doing it all over again to commit the next note to the machine's memory. It had taken three weeks to compose four bars of music. Three weeks ago, they said he was mad. Now they said he was a survivor, a hero, a genius who would not be defeated by physical constraints. His body might not work but his mind was still sharp.

Arturo's thoughts wandered back beyond the day, three weeks earlier, when the device arrived. He recalled the time six months before that, to the day the first machine arrived. This machine, once itself the thing of science fiction, was now fairly commonplace, allowing severely disabled patients the opportunity to "speak" by tapping letters on a screen with a probe attached to the head. He remembered the emotion of being able to communicate effectively for the first time since the accident. He remembered vividly one of the first sentences he had constructed on the device: 'will I ever play again?' He remembered the doctors had given him platitudes rather than concrete assurances. But deep down inside, even though he was aware of the extent to which his body was mangled and deformed, he knew he would play again.

His mind drifted further back - to the day of the accident itself. He was on his way to perform Rachmaninov's Concerto No.2 at the Royal Albert Hall. He was one of the most gifted pianists of his generation, and that evening's performance was to be the pinnacle to date of his embryonic career. His driver didn't see the taxi as it jumped the lights and embedded itself into the passenger side of the car, the side where Arturo was sitting. It was instant. His spinal cord was severed immediately. His arms and legs lifeless from that moment forward.

The doctors conceded that he was making progress, albeit slowly. This gave him great hope, kept him going. Made him survive each day. Made him fight for the talking device. Seeded the idea in his mind of the composing machine. He didn't even know if such a device could be made, if the software even existed, but he was determined to have one. And his persistence paid off, for here he was, nearly a year on from the accident, four bars into his masterpiece.

The doctors had asked him, 'Why are you doing this, why are you putting your body through so much torture, just to get a few musical notes onto a computer screen?'

He answered, with his head frenetically tapping the probe onto the screen, 'I can't play, but I can see music in my head. And if I can see it, I can write it. And if I can write it, one day I will play it. That's what keeps me going. One day, I will play it.'

WHY I WRITE (PAST, PRESENT AND FUTURE)

'Come and write,' they said. 'It'll be fun,' they said. 'It'll unlock the imagination and open up a hitherto undiscovered world, limited only by the bounds of unconscious thought, and take you on a magical journey of enlightenment and enrichment.' OK, I made that last bit up, but I was definitely up for writing and fun, and I was game to see where it would take me.

I had other needs to be met too. I needed to get out of the house on Monday evenings. I wanted to meet new people and mix with souls both likeminded and otherwise. I needed something that would challenge me cerebrally and stir the old grey matter into action. I wanted to write something that wasn't a bloody technical report or university coursework. I wanted something therapeutic, a safe place to vent feelings and express emotions. Somewhere to dissipate my existential angst and maybe provide an answer to the eternal question: what does it all mean? And yes, I wanted to go on that magical journey. I needed some escapism in my life, something to get me away from the humdrum drudgery of everyday life and take me to a place that only existed in my head.

And so how has that all worked out? I'm out of the house on Mondays. Tick. I've met likeminded souls. And otherwise. Tick. The brain cells have been shocked into life. Tick. I've written. Tick. It's been therapeutic at times. Tick. And as for that journey? This term has taken me to a secret side of London along the Regent's Canal. It's shown me the horrors of the humanitarian crisis in the Middle East. It's taken me back to the Gunpowder Plot. I've seen stunning autumnal colours and I've felt the cold of winter. I've revisited my 1970s childhood and I've seen the light and dark sides of Christmas. So yes, I think it has done what it said on the tin. And more.

'So, are you coming back next term?' the tutor asked.

'Maybe,' I said, 'what can I expect?'

'It'll be fun,' she said. 'It'll unlock the imagination and open up…'

'OK. I get the picture. Sign me up.'

'You'll get out of it whatever you want to get out of it,' the tutor said with a wry smile on her face. 'And the more you put in, the more you'll get out.'

I headed off into the Christmas break with a head full of thoughts. Sure, I wanted to write more, but what did I really want from the coming term? What were my expectations, not just from the writing course, but from writing *per se*, in the coming term and beyond?

Certainly, all the boxes that had been ticked at the end of the previous term needed ticking again. And I definitely wanted to go on another incredible journey through space and time. But I had a sense of wanting more. Yes, I had challenged myself last term. The eulogy I'd written for the dead Syrian baby was powerful and painful and had come from a place beyond my imagining. But I needed to push myself harder. I often tell people that the magic only happens when they step outside their comfort zone, and that's where I need to be. Not coasting along in the safety of whimsical and mildly amusing observational pieces (like this one), but taking myself to places I have never been and of which I have no first-hand experience, places where I'm uncomfortable, or fumbling in the dark, and writing from there. I want to experiment with different writing styles. The term of poetry that we did was a revelation for me. I never imagined I would have a gift for it, nor that I would enjoy it. But enjoy it I did. Not only did I write poetry, but I began to read it. I even managed to watch it being performed live. So, I would like a similar experience with other genres and writing styles. I am hopeless at writing descriptive prose. I don't do horror. I've never composed a fictional bedroom scene – to be honest, they're not my forte in real life either - or pieced together a murder mystery. Children's stories are an alien life form to me. So, bring it on. All of it.

I want to go on more journeys. I want to write less from personal experience and more from the imagination. I want to put myself in unfamiliar scenarios in unknown landscapes with characters foreign to me, and just write.

So, this being the time for making resolutions for the coming twelve months, I hereby solemnly resolve to step out of my comfort zone in terms of new styles, different genres and previously unimagined scenarios and situations. Let's see where that takes me!

KATYA MORGAN

Katya Morgan has lived in the Abergavenny area all her life. She works as a health care assistant in Nevill Hall hospital. She has one teenaged son. She has enjoyed writing as a hobby for several years. She is also a keen amateur poet and has participated in open mic competitions for local charities. Katya was a student in Sharon Brace's writing class last year.

IT'S AUTUMN AGAIN

It's Autumn again, and in one way I'm happy to say goodbye to the summer. To see my son settled back in school. To get some routine and order back. To be able to clean my house without it becoming messed up no sooner than I have started. I'm looking forward to the cold, cosy nights, and putting the heating on. Getting my winter wardrobe out, exchanging summer dresses for woolly jumpers and cosy fur coats. Looking forward to Halloween, marvelling at the costumes the children wear today, as opposed to the homemade Halloween costumes of my youth - for example, black bin liners for witches and white sheets for ghosts.

Watching horror movies with my partner and cuddling into him pretending to be scared, rather than just craving affection. I'm looking forward to bonfire night fireworks lighting up the sky like jewels in a sea of black satin. The smell of toffee apples. Burgers, hot dogs, frying onions. Looking forward to taking my dog out for long leisurely walks, our feet crunching the dead leaves on the floor.

Starting to think about Christmas, what I need to buy, hoping I've enough money to tide me over. Feeling sad for the homeless, who are always there but, as the seasons become darker and colder, their plight seems worse. Feeling fortunate that, although my life isn't perfect, I have a roof over my head, food and shelter, and family and friends that love and care for me. I'm looking forward to the New Year, with spring the next season, bringing with it the promise of summer. As a child I always preferred Christmas Eve to the day itself, as to me, the promise and anticipation of something is often better than the reality.

MOBY AND THE BEANS

It's been six months since I came back to university. I'm in my second year. And am no longer living in halls. I now live in a shared house with three other students. Tim, Charlotte, and Moby. What can I tell you about my housemates? There's Charlotte, a drama student. Posh, horsey and into fine dining, she definitely likes the finer things in life. Tim, your typical rugger-bugger, also posh. The type who refers to girls as totty. Myself, Carys, your typical working-class Welsh girl. I'm studying English literature and I'd say I'm the most normal in the house. And lastly, Moby, who is one of the most unlikely students I know. I'm not sure why he's called Moby, probably because he's massively overweight. I think it has something to do with Moby Dick... didn't that have something to do with a whale? You would think I would know that, wouldn't you, considering I'm studying literature? Anyhow, Moby was studying computer gaming. And his hobbies consisted of sitting around playing computer games, drinking beer, and eating loads and loads of Heinz baked beans. There always seemed to be lots of green tins hanging around. Sometimes he'd eat the beans straight out of the tin... gross! He had this mate, Spud, who often came round to us with Moby. I'm not sure how he acquired his nickname - maybe because he has a love of jacket potatoes, or maybe because he has all the charm and appeal of a spud, I don't know. Anyway, he was always around too. The two of them sat on the sofa, playing games, drinking beer, and breaking wind. It certainly wasn't the university experience I had signed up for. Honestly, if I never see a tin of Heinz baked beans again it will be too soon. And seems I wasn't the only one. It was a couple of weeks ago now, coming back to our shared house to find Charlotte, bin liner in hand with a determined look on her face, going through the kitchen cupboards.

'What are you doing Charlotte?' I asked. She certainly wasn't one for housework.

'I'm getting rid of all these bloody tins of beans,' she protested. 'Honestly, I am sick to death of them. They're everywhere, and the smell that emanates from those two Neanderthals, it's a wonder the house doesn't require fumigation.'

'But they're Moby's, aren't they? Aren't him and Spud going to be cross?'

'I honestly don't care,' she said. 'I wish I had a bin liner big enough to throw *them* out. At least, if there's no beans in the house, they will get off their fat arses and go out. Tim and I are throwing a party, and Moby and Spud are not the right clientele.'

'Am I invited?' I asked, as no party had been mentioned to me.

Charlotte looked at me in a scrutinising way. 'I suppose so, just try and rein in that Welsh valleys girl-ness.' Honestly, she was such a snob, and, not for the first time, I wondered how I had ended up in a house-share with so many different-minded people.

'What do you mean?' I asked indignantly.

'You know, the way you talk, all that who's-coat-is-that-jacket. I'll-do-it-now-in-a-minute nonsense. My friends don't understand that kind of talk. We all talk properly - the Queen's English.'

'What, the yah-yah crowd,' I was about to say, 'who laughed and neighed like inbred horses?' As if on cue, to prove my point, Tim entered the room.

'Yah, Lottie,' he drawled. 'Have you collected all those ghastly beans?'

'I think so.'

'Yah, great, once we've got rid of their farting fuel, and got the oiks out, old Timbo can entertain all the top totty.'

'And plenty of eye candy for us gals,' tittered Charlotte.

'Alright,' I said. 'So, you've taken all their beans. But it doesn't mean you can throw them out for the night. It *is* their house too.'

'At least, it's Moby's house.' I added, as Spud spent so much time here, I sometimes forgot he didn't live here too.

'Oh, they'll be out alright,' Tim said. 'Trust me they won't be able to get in.'

What do you mean?' I asked again.

'Well, I heard Moby say he'd be at Spud's this evening, so I've paid a locksmith to come round and change the locks. There will be keys for you, me, and Lottie. Lottie didn't want to include you, but you're such top totty,' Tim smarmed, 'that I couldn't bear to turn you out. But do behave yourself at the party, Carys. Rein in that valleys, "up the workers" attitude, it can be very irksome.'

'Oh yah,' said Charlotte. 'Definitely.'

'Look,' I said, starting to get annoyed. 'I know Moby can be a dick at times. And, well, just not very appealing. But he lives here too. You can't just change the locks. He could go to the Dean and report us. We could be in serious trouble.'

'Let him try,' Charlotte said. 'My father is a governor at this university, a very important man. Puts a lot of money into this place. No!' she said in that self-assured way she had. 'He won't want to cross daddy.'

'What will you do with those beans, Lottie?' Tim asked.

'Throw them out in the rubbish,' she replied.

'No,' I said. 'Don't do that. I'll take them over to the Foodbank down the road.'

'Yes, good idea,' said Tim, thoughtfully. 'Oiks do love beans, and I have no objection to them eating them in their own trough, just not in my surroundings.'

So, it was decided I would be the one to take the beans to the Foodbank. But I wasn't going to take them just yet. For now, I would keep them in my room. There was something about all this that gave me a bad taste in my mouth.

Admittedly, I found Moby as annoying as everyone else, but you couldn't treat people like that. And I couldn't help thinking if I didn't, as Tim so elegantly put it, have "a cracking pair of jubblies" and a "desirable *derriere*," I would be chucked out in the cold too.

So, the locksmith came round later that evening and changed the locks. Tim handed us our keys. And I was told to prepare for the party, or the *soiree*, as Charlotte put it. What can I say about the party, except to say I felt as if I had wandered into the first-class lounge on a plane when it was clear I belonged in business class. In my whole time at uni, I had never been so aware of the class divide. The girls largely ignored me. And the lads only talked in the hope they could get into my knickers, as if knocking off a working-class, Welsh lass was something of a novelty. At about half ten, I could hear a loud knocking at the door, and Moby calling out.

'Guys, what's going on? I can't get my keys to work. Carys, Tim, Charlotte... anyone? Someone please answer the door.' As he continued to knock, the room burst into laughter. And as it did, I felt my blood boil. I hated bullies, always have. Suddenly the knocking stopped, and Moby, confused and angry, walked away. As he did, Charlotte opened the lounge window and shouted, as Princess Anne use to do to the press in her heyday, 'Naff off,' and once more, the room filled with laughter. Able to stand it no more, I went up to my bedroom and slammed the door. And as I sat on my bed, I realised I had two choices. I could do nothing. And that would make me as bad as them. Or I could do something about it. I chose the latter. I picked up my mobile phone, rang Moby and told him what had happened. To say he was annoyed was an understatement; I'd never seen him so steamed up. In fact, the only time I have ever seen him show any real emotion was when he was playing one of his games, or when his beans and beer had run out. I asked him if he could find somewhere to stay tonight. And I'd meet him in the pub tomorrow and we would hatch our plan of revenge. I met him the next evening and told him that Charlotte had also taken his beans and wanted to throw them out, but I had stopped her.

'I can't believe it,' he said. 'Why would anyone want to throw out my beans? What harm have they done?' I shrugged even though I knew their reasons. But I didn't have heart to tell him. What good was there in kicking somebody when they were already down?

'So, what we going to do Carys?' he asked.

'I know what we're *not* going to do.' I said. 'We're not going to take it. Just because they object to your beans, they can't throw you out.'

'Yeah, too right,' he said. 'And if they can do it to me, you might be next.'

I nodded in agreement. And then an idea hit me, a light bulb moment. Charlotte had said she was sick of being surrounded by beans.

'You know those beans, Moby?' I asked. How about you don't eat them all?'

'What do you mean?' he asked.

'How about we use some to decorate Charlotte and Tim's rooms? Put some in their shoes and their clothes' pockets. Then they'll know how it feels to be surrounded by beans.'

And that's exactly what we did. I cut a copy of my key and gave it to Moby. He moved back in that night. Charlotte and Tim seemed most displeased to see him back. But what could they say? He had every right to be there. But they both gave me dirty looks, as if I was a traitor. And that was fine. I didn't want to be part of their mean tricks and games. Now Moby and I had a few of our own. As they went upstairs to change, we delighted in their screams and protests of having their belongings drenched in beans.

That was a few weeks ago now. And since "Beangate," as I like to call it, the atmosphere in the house has been truly awful. Charlotte and Tim have decided to move out to a flat in a nicer part of the area. And Spud is going to move in here. And they are now looking for three other like-minded roommates. Moby has told me I'm very welcome to stay. But as luck would have it, two girls on my course are looking for a third to move in with them. And the best thing about them is they definitely don't belong in the yah-yah club, and they both share a hatred of Heinz baked beans.

MY FAVOURITE SEASON AS A CHILD

As a little girl I loved spring. Most children prefer winter - the thrill of Halloween, bonfire night and the wonder of Christmas. But for me it's always been Spring. Springs from when I was a child always seemed better. Whether it was just my imagination, or the way it really was, I can't say. But somehow the sun always shone brighter. And my already olive skin would turn a darker shade of brown just from being outside, playing. I miss that as an adult - you don't go outside with your friends playing made up games. Well I suppose you *could*, but people would think you were crazy. But when you're a child, no one judges you. You can be what you want to be. When you're a child your imagination works better. You can get lost in your fantasies in a way adults can't.

    I remember springs from when I was a child, playing out with my sister in the garden of our childhood home. We were both avid readers, fascinated by the books of Enid Blyton and her stories of elves and fairies, and magical lands at the bottom of the garden. At the end of our garden there was a well with steps leading down, like a wishing well. And as we began to play, we imagined there were fairies down there, and reality would mingle with fantasy, as we swore we could hear their tiny voices, and evidence of their footprints and things they may have left behind. One of us would try to convince the other that they'd caught sight of one. And the other one would want to believe. And that is why Spring was, and still is, my favourite season because it reminds me of a time when I was young and innocent and believed in magic and fairy tales. Sometimes, when I'm bogged down with the stress of adulthood, I wish I could go back to those innocent times. And when May comes, the beginning of Spring, the promise of Summer, it gives me a warm glow inside.

WHAT LIES BENEATH

What lies beneath this woman I see?

What lies beneath is a mystery.

Behind a smile and a made-up face

Lies a heart of steel, a soul of lace.

Scars that are deep,

Tormented demons that will not sleep.

Secrets of a haunted past

About a love that didn't last.

Haunted by years of abuse

She wishes she could turn those feelings loose.

Feelings of low self-worth and shame.

So many emotions,

Too many to name.

A little girl lost and alone

A woman who has lost her home

No possessions of her own.

Jumps out of her skin

From a beep from her phone.

A woman who runs from place to place

Hoping no-one recognises her face.

So, this lies behind

This woman I see.

Anxiety and misery.

MARTIN STOPFORTH

Martin Stopforth is a retired IT Project Manager who relocated to South Wales 4 years ago to be close to family. Ever since getting the writing bug from essay assignments at school, he has dabbled with writing when the demands of career and family have permitted. He has been fortunate enough to join various creative writing groups over the years. This has inspired him to try various formats, including flash fiction, poetry, memoir, and short stories. He is a writing serial offender who loves the fun of playing out with words.

AUTUMN MEMORIES

How did we get here, now?

With the fading of the light,

As the veins in the leaves harden

And life cracks under stout shoes.

There used to be treacle toffee

Stuffed into a brown leather satchel

With white pumps, and a fresh jotter.

A new term - elevated to a higher class, again.

There were fireworks to lighten the crisp, black sky

And sparklers radiating charmed enlightenment

To the smoking, hand warming fire of redundant leaves

Before immersing in that juggled hot chestnuts joy.

Later, the baton moved down the line

And the new child re-awakened the forgotten child.

As the parent became the author

Of the new memories for a young life.

The golden season blows away the bright young thing of summer

With browning and fading, and the searing wind.

Just a taster on the lips

Of the cold, darker days ahead.

Yes, there used to be treacle toffee

And fireworks, and family magic.

Now it's firmly our speckled autumn.

Just how did we get here, now?

AUTUMN'S OUTSIDE

Was it really only just a year ago,

When I sat and mulled about conkers,

And bonfires and juggling hot chestnuts –

Wading through the faded leaves to autumns past?

Just one bitter-sweet, scented year,

To cherry pick,

The best,

And bury beneath,

The rest.

Tearing through the seasons,

Like a guided, migrating flock.

With their clear aerial view

Of what lies below.

I see the feet and inches,

Of the long days passing.

As your mood grew darker,

With the shortness of the light.

The days, the slow, heavy days,

Of the tidal range of your mind –

Ebb and flow, ebb and flow,

Until darkness receded, at last.

And here we are wizened,

Hurtling into another autumn.

This time, dark outside,

But dazzlingly bright within.

CHRISTMAS IS LOOMING

Unfortunately, Christmas is looming large yet again. We all know this because, even though it's not yet October, the supermarkets have cleared away all the shelves they normally devote to useful items like magazines, stationery, books, paper clips, and even birthday cards. (God help you if you're unfortunate enough to have a birthday in the last quarter of the year – your cards will be the very dregs). To make room to usher in Christmas, the useful items have been shunted away (just where do they store it, I often wonder?)

    Unbelievable amounts of shiny, glittery stuff turn up. There's baubles and tinsel, and cards that shout 'Yo-ho-ho' when you poke Rudolf's alcoholic nose. Then there are all those yule logs and brandy butter, and endless blinkin' lights.

Crackers – well named – galore, and, of course, delightfully scented candles all vie for attention.

This year, I was perplexed by a new section in this phantasmagoria of dubious Christmas delights. The items looked rather like plastic pizza bases that had had the pizza removed in favour of some leaves swept up by a grumpy council street cleaner. Then on top was a crowning glory of odds 'n' sods candles that couldn't find any mates their own size and shape. I asked a shop assistant what on earth these things were.

'Ah,' he said, 'that's the candle garden section. They're this year's strongest sellers.'

'Who would you give one of those to?' I asked.

'Ah,' he replied, 'that's the real bonus; you can give one to anybody!'

Graced with this comforting sagacity, I purposefully walked as far away as possible. I soon found myself in pleasingly close proximity to the real Christmas cheer – the malt whisky section. After browsing this section of the supermarket for longer than would seem decent, I noticed I was being watched suspiciously by the sagacious shop assistant of candle garden fame. Perhaps he thought I had super-hero like olfactory skills – like Desperate Dan's ability to sniff bacon and egg into his mouth from a distant plate. Maybe he thought I could empty several bottles of the finest scotch, merely by inhaling them vigorously from nearby. Then again, perhaps he thought I was just an indecisive wino. He took the opportunity to demonstrate that he was not just a candle garden spotter.

'Ah,' he said, 'it'll be a whisky you're looking for.'

Given we were standing in the whisky section with our noses reverentially raised towards the "expensively beyond reach" top shelf, I had to admire his stunning powers of deduction.

'Aye,' I responded, noncommittally.

'Would it be a tipple for everyday enjoyment, or something more attuned to special occasions?' he asked.

'Everyday special occasions,' I said.

He gave me that look which indicated he was beginning to get the measure of me.

'So, would that be a Speyside or from the Isles?' he enquired.

'Yes,' I said, confirming he was indeed getting the measure of me.

'How about this one – it's a new line we've got in especially for Christmas. And it comes with a free box of cupcakes. You see, those clever marketing boffins have analysed all the purchasing patterns and discovered that blokes who buy whisky often also buy cakes. Presumably to ease the path of returning home with another bottle of delight.'

'Good enough – I'll take it, then,' I conceded.

So, I went home and produced the box of cupcakes.

'There,' I said to my better half, 'and it came with a free bottle of scotch.'

'You useless wet whelk. Do you honestly expect me to believe that?' she said.

'Not really,' I replied, triumphantly pouring myself a well-earned dram.

"CHRISTMAS CANCELLED" SHOCK

The future of Christmas looked uncertain last night when news emerged that Santa had tendered his resignation. Santa called an unexpected press conference at his North Pole Workshop at midday yesterday.

Despite the short notice, the press conference was packed with reporters and television crews from around the world. On the dot of twelve o'clock, Santa strode in and took his place at the podium. A complete hush immediately fell around the room, as Santa cleared his throat and took a deep draft from what appeared to be a very large glass of sherry. He surveyed the room, grimaced, and then commenced his address.

'Thank you all for coming along today, particularly at short notice and in such inclement weather,' he began. 'I stand before you now to explain why I am resigning as Santa.'

he paused while the crowd gasped in unison.

'I've been doing the job of Santa for over a thousand years now,' he said, stroking his long white beard for emphasis, 'and I just can't do it anymore.'

Santa went on to explain that, apart from the gargantuan task that the role entailed, he simply could no longer stomach all the mince pies mandated at each house he stopped at on Christmas Eve. Curiously, however, the accompanying shot of whisky at each house didn't seem to present a problem.

When pressed to explain the mince pie issue more clearly, he just said, 'Mary Berry.' It transpired that the global phenomenon that Mary Berry has become over the last few years has resulted in a totally uniform mince pie, world-wide.

'She's taken over,' he said. 'Everyone either bakes mince pies exactly to her recipe or buys her standard brand of them. There's just no variation anywhere in the world. And they're too sickly sweet – just like her! So, I'm resigning, as of now.'

Cries of horror and disbelief filled the room. Eventually, the hubbub died down and Santa agreed to take questions from the floor. The reporter from Time magazine expressed concern over the effect Santa's resignation would have on the world's little children. Santa was indignant, saying,

'Well, the kids' parents will just have to step up, won't they? Anyway, they always moan about how Santa gets all the credit at Christmas. Now they can take the credit themselves.'

The team of Elves in the room had little sympathy with this view, and clearly sided with the Time magazine reporter. The Chief Elf was moved to speak to the crowd.

'I'm The Chief Elf, and I speak for all Santa's Elves. To be honest, I don't really understand Santa's problem. I mean, fair do's and all that – I can't stand that Mary Berry woman, either – but her mince pies are fine.'

'Well, why don't you eat the mince pies then?' grumped Santa.

And that was the light bulb moment. The crowd put it to Santa that he could take the Elves with him on Christmas Eve to help deliver all the presents. That way, the Elves could eat the mince pies for him.

'Well, OK,' said Santa, 'but you're not having any of the whisky – that's for me.'

So, Christmas was saved at the eleventh hour.

Meanwhile, it is rumoured that Santa has secretly hatched a plan to create a superior mince pie to drive Mary Berry out of the market by next Christmas.

ENDLESS DAY

You know all about endless days, don't you?
Time spent with that one so loved.

When spirits soar to the top of the hill,
Ahead of the sluggish legs.

Or the long, indulgent, boozy lunch,
At that bijou restaurant marinated in memories.

Or the wellied stomp through the cracking fresh snow,
Before glugging mulled cider, bloom faced, by the crackling fire.

Or heading up to town, to buy those special, vital shoes,
And wear them to the enchanted old theatre.

Or the quiet, peaceful day at home,
Gently working through the backlog of undemanding tasks.

Or the ambling, rambling, unplanned day,
With serendipitous joy at what happens to unfold.

Yes, I knew about endless days, aplenty,
Until you were no longer there to share.

And now my days are no-longer-endless.
Just a monochrome empty space,
With the same end.

GLUE

You would never miss a chance to tell me when I was a boy
(Just on the off chance that I may have forgotten)
That epoxy resin is a man's best friend.

Your knowledge of glues was fabled throughout the district.
Everyone knew that if anything needed sticking together,
You were the man for the job, at once.

You held our family together with little more than just vinegar and brown paper,
As you fixed up the house with pungent pots of this and that,
And melded together all that needed constructing, or repair.

All the while, in a state of focused attention,
As your skills flowed outwards in a state of pure glee.

They could make good use of your cheerful talents and hard work now,
Here in this derisory hospital room,
With its rickety chairs, wobbly table, and cracked fruit bowl.

If only,

If only,

If only you could remember -

Even for just five minutes.

'Tell me, son, about all the things I used to love.'

GUMBO PIE

The coffin weighed heavily on his shoulder, mostly because he was taller than the other five coffin bearers. He had no idea who these four men and one woman were, nor why his father had stipulated they were to be the bearers of his coffin. Their names he knew from the will, but nothing more.

When he had arrived at the All Saints Chapel that morning, he was perspiring in his formal black suit. He had been alone and wondered whether he had come at the right time. He had been prodding his silver pocket watch to check that it was still working when there was a tap on his shoulder.

'Well, well. So, you really do exist after all,' she said. 'The old bastard always claimed he had a son in London, but nobody believed him. And now here you are, all in your English finery, meltin' in the New Orleans sun.'

'And to whom do I have the pleasure?' he asked.

'I'm Simone. And you won't be gettin' any pleasure here, I can tell you,' she replied, lighting up a cigarette. 'Funeral starts in ten minutes, at twelve o'clock sharp.'

He was glad of the confirmation, the pocket watch still being on UK time, as he examined it once again.

'Let me see that quaint old thing,' she said, reaching for the watch. She read out the inscription on the back. "Happy 21st My Dearest Son. Your Loving Father, Walter."

'*Dearest* Son, eh? So, there's probably others.'

It was a thought that had crossed his mind many times, especially now, as he eyed up his fellow pall bearers. His size eleven black leather brogue shoes kicked up dust on the gravel path leading to the faded wooden double doors of the mouldering Chapel.

He patted the inscribed champagne cork in his pocket, and, wondering who else had one, noticed there were only two people sitting inside the Chapel. He puzzled over the mention in his father's will of uncorking his destiny at the funeral. He popped a Polo mint into his mouth in a futile attempt to cool down.

The Preacher made up for the fact there were no eulogies by vehemently exhorting the sparse assembly to forthwith abandon a life of moral turpitude, while there was still time, and so avoid the fires of eternal damnation. Then he pushed the button to draw the curtain across the front of the coffin and despatch it along the clattering track into the furnace.

**

After the funeral, there had been no reception. Instead, Simone had suggested the two of them meet for dinner that evening.

'Hook up with me for a bite tonight. Ruby's Smoke House. It's tucked away at the back of Bourbon Street. Everyone knows it, so you'll find it easy enough. Eight o'clock, sharp.'

And with that, she had gone, along with his fellow pall bearers. The other two mourners also shambled off into the side streets, without a word. He made his way back to his colonial style hotel, showered and changed into his Hawaiian shirt, cargo trousers, loafer shoes, and baseball cap with a Ferrari logo. He carefully folded up the white shirt and black suit and put them away in his silver Samsonite roller case – biding their time, ready for the next departure. He cut his fingernails with his nail clippers and checked his hair in the mirror. He stretched at his neck, reflecting on how even a size seventeen shirt collar was now beginning to feel tight. Looking out over the wrought iron rail of his balcony, he sighted the neon sign of a bar, and then headed out to casually engage with the throbbing French Quarter.

At eight o'clock he rolled up at Ruby's Smoke House. It was obviously one of the places to go in town. Rammed and super-charged, it was full of New Orleans' finest and coolest – with plenty you'd love to have sex with, some you wouldn't, and others you just wouldn't know what you'd be getting until you opened up the lucky bag. Simone caught his eye and beckoned him over.

'Gotcha, Pearson. My, oh my, don't you look different from this morning.'

She was wearing a bright red velvet dress that apparently had been shrink wrapped onto her. Clearly, the dress maker had also been very economical with the amount of material required.

'Well, just look at you, too,' Pearson eventually managed.

They took a table on the veranda at the back, in the open air. He pulled out her chair and helped her to get seated. Next, he unfolded a napkin and gave it to her, and passed her a menu. Following her recommendation, he ordered the house special gumbo, followed by key lime pie. She agreed his suggestion to have Long Island Iced Tea for their drinks.

'Tell me, Pearson – you married or anything?' she asked.

'Fortunately, no woman's been stupid enough to stick with me for long enough for that to be an issue. How about you?'

'No, no, it's not for me – I'm having far too much fun,' she said. 'You're some kind of computer geek, aren't you?'

'You could say that I guess' he replied, 'I run a software company. We specialise in security systems for banks. Making sure all the money in the world stays where it's supposed to be.'

'That should be lucrative, then?'

'Very. I do just fine out of it.' He took another mouthful of his gumbo. 'Good choice this gumbo, really yummy!'

'Yummy? You can only get away with that in your English accent!'

He forced a partial smile. 'You were my father's lawyer, right? Did you know him well?'

'That may take a little while to explain.' She smiled broadly in return. 'I was his lawyer for quite some time. And it evolved over the years into helping to manage his assets. And, my god, did he have some money! He was very, very successful. We needed to get together a lot to look after his portfolio.'

'What was he like? I really want to know. You see, he left my mother and me just after my twenty-first birthday. That was almost thirty years ago. I never heard from him again. Just nothing, until you got in touch about the funeral and the will.'

'Oh, that must have been hard on you. He was a very complicated man. Charming, handsome, enigmatic, and stunningly brilliant. But he certainly had a dark side, though. He was totally ruthless, and his downfall was his weakness for pretty, petite, youngish, professional, black women.' She paused. 'Yes, I know what that look you're giving me means. Dead right, women just like me.'

'Sorry. I didn't mean to be so crass. But' - he hesitated - 'you were involved?'

She emptied the Long Island Iced Tea – her second. 'That's another deep question. We started out on purely a professional basis. Your father had a well-earned reputation for being a one for the ladies. Rashly, I introduced him to some of my girlfriends, and he charmed his way around the entire circuit. They said he *really* knew how to please a woman. Most of the men I've known hee and haw and rub at you like they're trying to sand down an old wooden sideboard. What my girlfriends said niggled away at me. Walter's will is all about his Wellingborough Trust. I set it up for him and moved pretty much all his assets into it. He had very little money left after his fortune had been moved into the Trust, and he couldn't afford my fees anymore. So, we came to an arrangement, if you know what I mean. Boy, was it worth it.'

'Oh, I see,' he said.

They finished up their key lime pies and ordered more drinks.

'Do you mind if I have a cigar, kind of in honour of the old man?' he asked.

'Sure. So long as it's a big one. I like a man who smokes a big cigar.'

He took a Romeo y Julieta Churchill cigar from its tube, clipped it, and carefully lit up. They were on to their fourth Long Island Iced Tea. It was time for the burning questions.

'Who were the other guys at the funeral?'

'I wondered when you'd ask,' she said. 'Your father had many liaisons over the years. None lasted too long - women would kick him out when they realised he was doing the fandango all over town. Those guys are the unfortunate side effects of your father's appetites.'

'They're sort of my brothers, then?'

'Yes. And they're all cited in the will. And each one got a Bollinger champagne cork, embossed with three different numbers. I guess you must have got one, too?'

'Yes. It arrived in a little box just after you first contacted me,' he said.

'Good. Your father made a short trip to London not long before he died. He wouldn't tell me why, except to say those numbers are the combination for a safety deposit box at the Bernstein Bank in London.'

He was pleased and couldn't conceal a slight grin. This confirmed what he suspected from the information he had hacked from Simone's computer earlier in the week. Just the five corks, and he knew all the numbers.

'You know, you really do remind me of your father,' she said.

They looked deeply into each other's eyes and smiled.

The terrace of Ruby's Smoke House looked out towards a jazz venue. It sounded like Dr. John and Satchmo themselves had teamed up to make timelessly beautiful music. It wafted out languorously into the night air and mingled with Pearson's cigar smoke, in a tightly embraced, sensuous, slow dance.

***

The following day, Simone had called a meeting in her office for Pearson and his newfound brothers "at twelve o'clock, sharp."

By noon, Pearson was already halfway across the Atlantic in the First-Class compartment of a British Airways flight to London. He had re-arranged his itinerary early that morning. Now he was starting on his second bottle of champagne as he reached for his ever-present book, "The Rise and Fall of Microsoft." He re-read with glee the chapter about how the founders of Microsoft achieved world domination through an unshakeable belief that they could do *anything* they wanted to.

LEGS

In the early days, when I was on my wibbly toddler's legs,
I was masterfully ignorant, and blissfully simple.
Moving on swiftly through the cheeky monkey stage,
I grew into those legs until a teenager finally emerged.
An unruly, grumpy creature – truly a bear with a sore head.

Eventually shedding that skin
A fully formed adult burst forth
With the heart of a lion, to challenge the world.

Life flowed uphill like a mud slide,
With exotic experiences to develop the memory of an elephant.
Wisdom poured onto one side of life's see-saw,
While success mandated an old toady grew fat on the other.

All the while, the legs buckled under the weighty strain.
But the legs cupboard had already been raided one last time,
And I was on my last pair.

A small price to pay for the well-oiled see-saw,

With a sly old fox sat at one end,

And a wise old owl balanced at the other.

NEW YEAR RESOLUTIONS SYNDROME

New Year has a nasty habit of coming along each year with the attendant threats to kick start a new, better life. This better life is usually based on improving me and is recklessly predicated on actually being feasible.

This New Year, just like countless New Years before, I took a stiff drink and declared that I would eat less, drink less alcohol, and get more exercise. For good measure, I also unwisely threw in that I would endeavour to have a more cheerful outlook on life.

It was a faultless start, immediately followed by a New Year's Day of excessive feasting, drinking and total lethargy. January 2nd came along with a sore head, which kicked the cheerfulness into touch. Things could only improve from that baseline.

In contrast, the rest of the first week was a raging success. Most of the Christmas fare had already been consumed, so I could reduce the overall intake by at least a few percent. This mostly manifested itself by sitting on the settee, eating just three of the residual mince pies each day, washed down by a few sherries. After a few days, all the remaining supplies had been consumed.

This is where the exercise kicked in. There was a burgeoning need to get some more supplies in. Spurning the car, I walked to the local shops and staggered home as a beast of burden. I had bought good, disturbingly healthy food. And no booze.

I was clearly on a roll (and not a Swiss one, for once).

So, I kept on rolling and rolling in this way, getting cheerful in a halo of self-righteousness.

It was time to take stock of matters. I was succeeding! Or, at least, I thought so, until I had to admit to myself that I was succeeding only by following government strategy to "only set targets that cannot be measured nor disputed."

Marvellous!

ORIGINAL SIN

Do not do that my child.

It is my will that you must obey.

Do not take heed of your wayward temptations.

It is my will that you must obey.

Do not do that forbidden violating thing.

It is my will that you must obey.

Do not question why it must be so.

It is my will that you must obey.

Do not contrive a reason to excuse your desires.

It is my will that you must obey.

Do not ask the purpose of my creations.

It is my will that you must obey.

Do not ask for more than I gave you.

It is my will that you must obey.

Do not give in to that evil serpent's goading.

It is my will that you must obey.

Do not forever ruin the fruits of paradise.

It is my will that you must obey.

Do not damn all with your original sin.

Do not.

SHEDDIE ALERT

As usual, Nigel could hear his wife's voice filling the room before she actually made an appearance.

'Get out of that chair, you lazy bugger.'

He reflected on how she always knew, from afar, when he was sitting in his favourite armchair. Had she secretly bought a smart cushion, with a sensor that triggered an App alert on her ever-present phone?

'Look, winter's over, so you've no more justification for being a sloth. Get up and do something,' she said.

'Spring into action, you mean?' Nigel said.

'Precisely!' she confirmed.

Having stood up to show willing when his wife had appeared, he felt forced to sit down again under the weight of her direction. He had to admit to himself that even he felt moved by Spring. Unidentifiable triffids were on the march in the garden again. It was light very early and insisted on staying that way until so late it upset his post teatime snooze routine. There was the strange whiff of blossoms, and birds singing interminably. He was utterly surrounded by spontaneous activity.

After much careful consideration, he decided to address Spring in his customary fashion. He headed for the shed. It was, of course, a wonder house of the last year's unfulfilled ambitions. Paint pots that had lain undisturbed since he managed to avoid painting the house due to the poor, wet, summer. A bike that needed repair – a status worsened by a decade of neglect. Then there was the collection of wood in various shapes and sizes, together with a cart load of screws and nails and brackety things, and an arsenal of the finest handyman tools, worthy of a fine handyman. Light years too good for Nigel, though.

He stared at the rusting screws and decided he would – definitely this time – make the bookcase that he had abandoned at the outline planning stage several smaller waistbands ago. After succumbing to a cup of tea and grubbing around the boxes and shelves and old tobacco tins, he found the original design plan. It had come free with "Bookcase Builders Monthly" magazine that his wife had optimistically bought for him, years ago.

Inspired by the bright, natural light shining through the shed window onto the now faded bookcase design blueprint, Nigel resolutely resolved to procrastinate until the Summer would come along and make the shed too hot to work in.

SQUARE SUN

When you challenged me to a duel
Because I didn't think like you
It made me sharpen my wits
And polish my pistol.

When you said I talked codswallop
And never let facts influence my bias
It made me read all the broadsheets
And scrub up my fish kettle.

When you pointed out my shortcomings
Because I always made a mess of things
It made me enrol on a DIY Master Class
And varnish my yardstick.

When you cried out I was stupid
Because I seemed to know nothing
It made me do general knowledge quests
And dust off my Encyclopaedia Britannica.

When you said I was useless

Because I was an emotional pygmy

It made me do therapy

And sand down philosophy out loud.

When you said you were leaving

Because I was a totally inadequate specimen

It made me despair for my future

And clean up my square globe.

The world is still square

With the sun going round it

Nothing makes sense, anymore

As far as I know.

THE RESOLUTIONS CONUNDRUM

To paraphrase Oscar Wilde, I don't know who to feel sorry for more: those who achieve their New Year resolutions, or those who don't. The basic premise is clearly idiotic. At an arbitrary point in your life, set yourself an unrealistic target to achieve a dubious outcome that even you have not bought in to. So, I suggested to myself the following anti-resolutions:

1. Be happier with imperfections.
2. Ignore all advice.
3. Pursue a life of unabashed hedonism.

Whereas this sounded remarkably simple, it turned out to be just as challenging as the usual "get thin, get fit, and turn yourself into an upstanding, teetotal pain in the arse" type of resolutions.

I started to work on my imperfections. The trouble was there were not enough of them to make the effort worthwhile. I was already perfectly happy with my gleefully few shortcomings. With that one ticked off long before January was even over, I moved to the next one. But I couldn't remember what it was (poor memory being another of my most satisfactory imperfections).

What I did remember, however, was that someone once advised me to write everything down just in case I forgot it. In this case, I had written it down, so I looked it up and it said, "Ignore all advice." Clearly, I had failed on that one, then.

Next up was the one about hedonism. I thought about this for a while and finally settled upon realising this through an endless series of Bacchanalian orgies. The trouble was there didn't seem to be many of them in progress in my neighbourhood, however hard I searched.

So, I gave up (always a good outcome), and reflected for a while. Failing to come to any earth-shattering conclusions (another of my agreeable shortcomings), I gave up on that, too.

It seems my anti-resolutions turned out to be the same mirages as my self-flagellating resolutions of old. Hey, ho – back to the future!

THE WAR TO END ALL WARS

Billy woke early that morning to a sound he had not heard for many years now. It was silent. Yes, silent! No battery of huge artillery firing, no whistle of shells overhead, no shouting sergeants, no men cursing, moaning, or screaming.

It wasn't just quiet in his room, it was clean, too. No trench mud anywhere in sight. From his cheap hotel room Billy could just make out the top of the Eiffel Tower in the distance. That was where he had spent the previous evening – revelling with the thronging, joyous crowds. Everyone was in a state of disbelief that the war was finally over. The "war to end all wars", they had said. We all hope to God that will be true. Well, it would be true if the crowds last night had their way - fuelled on Gauloises and bottle after bottle of liberating red wine. Oh, last night! A sense of hope, relief, optimism. You could see it in the faces, hear it in the hearty shouts and the songs, and feel it in the air.

And Maggie. Ah, that Maggie. She was making her way back home, too. Billy was reeling from how their chance meeting last night had lifted him. A feeling he didn't recognise – couldn't explain. And she had agreed to meet him again, today, for lunch.

***

'I can't believe we've never been back here before now,' said Maggie, after the passer-by had taken the photograph of them together, against the backdrop of the Eiffel Tower.

'No, and it still looks the same, which is more than can be said for us,' Billy replied. 'But I can still do this,' he said, lifting her into his arms for a kiss.

'There, you see. I've put on knowledge, not weight, in the last twenty years,' she said, smiling.

After the war, Maggie had stayed with nursing. She was now a matron, even though she hadn't gained the portentous figure normally associated with that role. She had never lost that kindness and open-spirited curiosity which had so enraptured Billy on the first night they had met, at this very spot. Billy, on the other hand, had found it difficult to repatriate after the war. He had been only sixteen when he had joined up in 1915, so had no trade to return to when back in England. He had spent most of their married life in and out of temporary labouring jobs. The worry lines on his face were as broad as his biceps.

'The war brought us together, but now that Hitler maniac is arming Germany, getting ready to have another go,' Billy said, 'and no damn stupid politicians can see it, except Churchill.'

Privately, Maggie agreed, but didn't want to say so. She chose instead to lead Billy over to the queue for the lift up the tower, hoping to see better horizons.

THINGS CAN ONLY GET WORSE

There was no fancy coat of arms
Nor poncy Latin motto.
Just a family guiding principle
That "Things Can Only Get Worse."

My father revered this so dearly,
As his father had before him,
That when he was gone
I had it inscribed on his stone.

"Things Can Only Get Worse"
And so, it came to pass,
When the gravestone cracked
And life became hacked.

My car caught fire.
My soufflé dire.

My investments crashed.
My health dashed.

My optimism lied.

My cat died.

My wife skedaddled.

My youth's addled.

My job redundant.

My holiday repugnant.

My roof collapsed.

My drinking relapsed.

So here I am, years along,

And learn, too late,

That, after this, "Things Can Only Get Better."

THREE STEPS TO CHRISTMAS HEAVEN

There is a very special type of Christmas Shop. You've all seen one – they lurk on most high streets. They pop up shortly before Christmas and, thankfully, pop down again immediately after Christmas. To give a clue, they are invariably called "The Christmas Shop." They hold a vast stock of junk, tailor-made for an instant – and disposable – Christmas. On the face of it, they are a trading outlet created by the mind of a cracking entrepreneur. In reality, they're most probably a money laundering vehicle for an opportunist criminal consortium.

One of the key lines they carry is the meaningless, inspirational phrase etched onto a bit of old wooden plank salvaged from derelict sheds in Wolverhampton. Being up-cycled and sourced from Wolverhampton undoubtedly adds to their authenticity, patina and, of course, inflated price. This year's best seller boasts the inscription: "Whoever Digs the Deepest, the Deepest Digs."

Running a close second in their best seller list is the Big Foot Single Slipper. It is like Siamese twin slippers that have never been separated since birth. It's just one big, furry man (or woman) trap. Absolutely guaranteed to see off your doddery old great aunt, when she tries to walk in it, and falls flat on her face.

And let's not lose sight of the Inflatable Santa. The best model is the deluxe, self-inflating, seven-foot high version. Yo-ho-ho has never been so good. Enjoy the unbridled merriment as it gets in the way of watching your Christmas telly (thankfully, though, blocking the sight of Bloody Mary Berry). Every home really should have one, or even two!

So, for the perfect Christmas, get down to your local Christmas Shop now, while there's still time!

WRITE TO KNOW YOURSELF

Many years ago, the actor Peter Ustinov was being interviewed on T.V. by Michael Parkinson. When asked whether he liked to be interviewed, Ustinov replied that he did, as it helped him to understand what he was thinking. This concept lodged itself like a small wooden splinter into the preternatural hinterland of my memory, where I trip over it again and again, as the years roll by.

The most recent of the evolving and disparate chapters of my life has been yet another relocation to a part of the country with which I am not familiar. This time it has been to a wonderful area in South Wales.

The process of relocating, and re-assimilating into a new environment, has become a habit through the persistence of previous memory. This time, however, the feelings of displacement and general malaise have been both disturbing and perplexing in equal measure. No amount of time and rational analysis had brought any absolution. It was clearly time to try to extract 'the Ustinov splinter' and interview myself.

Disconnected thoughts would enter my head, as they leaked randomly and sporadically from the memory vault. I took to writing these down.

After quite some time, these jottings began to look like the photos and incident notes pinned to a board in a Police CID murder investigation control room. The patterns and connections had to be determined, sifted, and sorted, and affirmed or discarded. Just like a murder investigation, the motives had to be established. The motives behind my disquiet needed to be unearthed. As the interrogation progressed, these motives slowly evidenced themselves as the pre-requisite factors needed for a sense of belonging.

My original sense of belonging had been established in childhood, many years ago. But this had become irrevocably damaged with changes in time, location, circumstances, family, and friends. The grit belonging in my grazed knees was simply no longer to be found, however hard it may be sought.

Clearly, the foundation factors of belonging could not be re-established – their substitutions would need to be constructed.

YELLOW BRICK ROAD

There are magisterial places that are neither here nor there,

Way up on high, or streaming out to distant sea,

On exotic shores beyond my greatest reach,

Or just around the corner.

There are no yellow brick roads, nor maps to guide me now,

No exorbitant bribe or bold travel agent can take me there again,

To that marvellous land, eroded with implacable time,

Fragmented in blue shards of impenetrable ice –

Some of it now fabled, some densely real.

The history of a lifetime, alluring,

Mocking that I have never wanted to be alone.

JULIE TAYLOR

Julie Taylor, a retired history teacher, recently returned to Abergavenny having spent a large part of her life in Bedfordshire. She has one son and shares care of her elderly mother with her sister. Julie has harboured a lifelong interest in writing and was one of the original members of the writing group.

CHRISTMAS

As he washed down the last mince pie with a final glug of port, Arthur told himself that it had been quite the best Christmas.

There are those who say old age is a gift, a pilgrimage, but if it was a gift, Charles Lawson neither wanted nor needed it.

It had been Charles' dream to be forever young. He so admired himself. He was an aspiring peacock from his fedora to his feet.

He was, in some ways, rather tragic. His mother, at forty-three, was sent into hospital to remove what the gynaecologist had thought was a massive ovarian cyst – which turned out to be Charles.

His father was a vicar, who claimed to have had a vision of the Virgin Mary.

DELIRIUM

It is six o'clock on an April morning. I open my eyes. There is never a moment when a hospital slumbers. The nurses are forever on their rubber-soled feet. If someone is very ill, as this morning, the curtains are drawn, the light is shaded, and the whispered conversations are terse. A life on the edge.

The junior doctor's eyes are glazed, and half hooded through lack of sleep. Her shift has not ended yet. She takes my hand and yawns as she searches for a vein. My veins in the back of my hand are hiding, but she catches one and the needle is in. It looks shaky to me, but she has gone. It will do for now.

The compulsory shower is soothing, and, in my mind's eye, I see myself, in my bed at home, unencumbered. The trappings of monitors and the sounds of the high-pitched bleep are yet to come. Oops! I watch the slithering needle fall onto the shower floor.

I reclaim my bed and note that most of the patients are still asleep, but one or two are beyond sleep and in pain and try to muffle their groans in case they wake a sleeper. I see the NHS gown sitting on the bed looking forlorn. It is anonymous. If you look at it in a pile of gowns, you will not recognise it. These NHS uniforms help to conceal your profile and personality. Now I feel anonymous – and afraid.

The curtains are around me while I stretch and try to move my big toe on the bed. There is a rustling, and a man appears. He is young. When a doctor comes to see you there is an aura which follows.

'Hello there. I'm an anaesthetist and I'm called Dr. Alexander. I will be assisting the senior consultant anaesthetist during your kidney transplant.'

'Why?' I say. 'Isn't it usually one anaesthetist for most operations?'

'Transplants are complex, and we try very hard to have the best conditions we can. After all, the patient has been ill for some time, like you. We need to prioritise your care while the operation is proceeding, and we look at the monitors and vital signs and alert the surgical team to any changes. We call it a "brace".'

'A brace of pheasants? Or brace yourself?' I said. 'Or a brace of anaesthetists?' I was mumbling to myself. 'No braces, your trousers come down. Brace in an aircraft spells disaster.' Well that's me told. All I know is that I have two anaesthetists and they will be watching me like hawks.

A stout porter comes to navigate the bed from the ward with me in it. Three identical corridors later and we reach the theatre block. The ante room is crowded. At least three people. They check my identity on my wristbands and note my red band for allergies. Without a whisper or a by your leave, I fall asleep.

I open my eyes. I am on a trolley. I see Patrick, one of the transplant doctors. He looks at me with concern. Something is wrong.

'Julie, what are you doing?'

I open my mouth to speak and I cannot talk. I open my mouth wider and there is no sound. I panic. I start to sweat. I try to move my lips and with my hands I give a big effort to grasp my tongue, but to no avail. My hands are floppy, and I am harnessed to the trolley with the paraphernalia that accompany me post-surgery. I feel something like a stream of fluid exiting my mouth. I am told that it is saliva.

My eyes are frightened. They flutter but I don't fit or faint. My tongue contorts and does a jig. I am babbling like a newborn. Oh, my Lord! If I have no speech, I can't talk. I am silent or grunting or making glugging sounds, and I am striving to send a signal to the receptors in my yawning brain.

'Stop this *immediately!*'

Nothing is happening.

'Do something!'

Patrick is focusing. His speciality is the kidneys, not neurology. He tells me I am going to have a CT scan. I am withering. I feel so small and very afraid.

Two young female orderlies come to my trolley. They are at the threshold of their lives and are full of eagerness. They are going to take me to the CT scanner. I am quiet now and my mouth is closed. Whatever is going on with me?

I have a *eureka* moment, but it is quite dreadful. I am known for my meandering talking, turning into another *cul-de-sac* of speech. Most of my friends are good editors. Ten minutes of speech is swiftly executed.

I have clamped my mouth. I feel a dribble. It is constant and continuous, and I am ashamed of it. It is another sign of loss of control.

In the scanner room, the orderly called Daisy brings the trolley to the edge of the scanner and the two of them move me over. It is swift and painless. The blonde orderly gives me a straw and holds the glass of water in the right place to make it easier for me to drink. She has been sorting the monitors and making a comfortable place for me on the trolley. At some point I think of daisies, and chains of daisies, and cows called Daisy, and I stray to mad cow disease, or locked-in syndrome, which I might have as I am wed to several machines. Kidney transplant delirium, now that's a thought as I fall back asleep…

Someone is interfering with my eyes. I screw up my eyes and it tickles. I give a mighty shout.

'Who is this man? Who is bending over me?'

'Professor Dudley. Your speech has returned, clearly.'

'Probably opiates, I think,' said the professor, shaking his head.

USC TIWARI

THE DANCER

Roberto looked at his Mama, his beautiful Mama, yet held his hands out in gentle exasperation. His father, Pietro, continued to enjoy his pasta con vongole, keeping out of the possible argument that might start its rumbling. But Pietro was looking now and again at his pretty young daughter, Carmella, of fourteen years - so young - who waited, a little anxiously, by the kitchen door, thinking, 'my brother is so sweet and kind. Nearly every Saturday, he takes me to the dance hall, and then later returns to take me home, for my safety, and peace of mind for Mama and Papa.'

'OK Mama, last time, the dance hall will have to be closed in couple of weeks' time... You know it is difficult already and soon there will be a strict curfew and the thugs will really be prowling the streets. They cannot be cautioned, or be touched by the weak *polizia*, who themselves are fearing for their own safety, by these marauding gangs, paid by the corrupt government.'

His Mama knew this was the last chance her sweet, pretty daughter would be able to try for the dance school classes next year, and really wanted Roberto to be with her, to be her partner in the practice steps. Usually, the girls partnered each other, guided by their teacher. She would call the pattern of the steps. But tonight, he might be persuaded to come into the hall and at least enjoy the music. She knew he was a good mover, with nimble feet, as he tripped and slid along the counter aisle, as the bakery radio played the latest songs and popular dance rhythms, even carrying trays, filled with hot-from-the-oven loaves and tasty ciabattas.

Usually, as Carmela and Roberto took the twenty-minute walk to the hall, one of Roberto's two friends would join them. A quiet, kind boy, Angelo was really fond of Carmella, but said nothing. Roberto guessed, but did not tease him, and would casually say that soon his little sister would tire of always being with her big brother. Roberto was two months shy of his eighteenth birthday. Tonight was the last night for the dance classes. Roberto' s friends were waiting for Carmella and him, so they all walked in a group to the hall.

On arrival at the hall, the music was really blaring out a new style that had everyone's feet moving infectiously. They all went inside to see what was happening. Carmela saw her other friends, already tentatively tapping out the rhythms, and their young teacher came over to welcome them, inviting the young men to join. She said tonight would be a free dance time, and to move as the music made you feel.

On becoming accustomed to the flickering lights from the twinkling glitterball, Roberto properly saw Carmella's dance teacher, Maria, for the first time. She was young and she was stunning - why on earth hadn't he gone into the hall before? He had an image in his head, that "teacher" equated with "old", really old, like his schoolteachers, who in fact even now were only a few years senior to his beautiful mother.

As the evening of music and dance, fun and laughter, drew to a close, Roberto managed to catch the last dance with Maria and, to the delight of his friend, the lucky stars shone on Angelo, as he asked Carmela for the last dance and she shyly but graciously accepted.

Then, when the music had faded, the evening had come to a close, and the lights were fully-on in the hall, a sudden aggressive banging started from outside the main door. Glass windows were heard being smashed. Before the young men in the hall had a chance to regroup and go towards the door, about ten to fifteen angry, aggressive young males, with wooden clubs and knives, burst into the hall. The intruders lashed out at the young men, who tried to duck, not always succeeding. Some of the girls ran to Maria, who gathered them as best she could behind her. One of Roberto's friends ran to them, trying to provide some shielding. Then the noisy aggression of the thugs lessened, until one could almost hear a pin drop. Roberto, alone, was standing in the middle of at least six of the thugs. The rest of the thugs had rounded up Roberto's other friends, along with their female partners.

Roberto immediately recognised the gang's ringleader. He had sometimes come to his father's bakery and been aggressive and rude, touching the fresh bread and snarling out political obscenities that he clearly did not understand. All he knew was symbols and colours. The political landscape in Parma was rapidly changing, and with the victory of the extreme right-wing pressure group, and the subsequent demonstrations, these random - yet at times, personal - attacks were on the increase. Roberto was targeted by this thug because of the poster his father had placed in the bakery window, simply exercising his democratic right to express and show his allegiance to his choice of political party. This had incensed the thug, and his anger was at boiling point when Roberto's father had told him to leave the bakery, because of his aggressive behaviour and foul language in front of the customers.

Now the thug stood, club in hand, screaming at Roberto that he was a "poofter" - obscene, unclean. Why? Because he danced and strutted around like a stupid bitch of a female. Roberto's friends ran towards the small circle of thugs trying to pull them away but were beaten back. At the same time the ringleader was smashing the club into Roberto's legs, really hard, until one heard bones crack. Roberto slumped to the floor, like a rag doll, and the final blows rained down on his back with a dull, heavy thud. He lay motionless, hands bruised and bleeding from trying to fend off the blows.

Carmela was distraught and reaching out to comfort her brother, but someone whispered to her to wait, and try to be still. As difficult as the situation was, the thugs may not be finished with their hateful mayhem. The ringleader turned to look at them all and sneered, jeering 'commie bastards' at them. He spun round to walk towards the door, club swinging, snapping his fingers for his pack to follow. He stopped in his tracks and pulled out a grubby piece of paper and flung it to a member of the gang as he passed Roberto, who was grimacing in pain, but not calling out. The thug flung the piece of paper on top of Roberto, and the gang stamped out of the hall, each with one arm held high in a grotesque salute. The ringleader brought up the rear and shouted, 'no more dancing for you, you commie poofter.'

As the door banged shut, they all rushed to Roberto, but Carmela, in desperation, could not read the paper through her tears. Angelo took the scrap in his hand and saw the Nazi symbol emblazoned across the whole page with Il Duce's stupid face in the corner.

It was nearly Christmastide, 1939.

AND FINALLY, A GROUP EFFORT

CHRISTMAS WORKSHOP POEM

Silent landscapes sprinkled with white.

Excited children, eyes shining bright.

Holy trees, mistletoe, tinsel, and bows.

May this season's wishes be bright as Rudolph's nose.

Many your world become enveloped in a blanket of snow,

Allowing great love and joy this Christmas time to flow.

And don't forget – wherever you are in the atmosphere,

The voice of Sir David – his message to us is to recycle our plastic without any fuss.

But it is Christmas and time to be joyous and merry,

Watch endless telly, but not bloody Mary Berry.

Abergavenny, December 7th, 2018.

Contributors in order:

    Rosie

    Vicky

    Emma

    Carolyn

    Martin